CLASH
OF HEARTS

CLASH OF
HEARTS

•

Darlene Gardner

AVALON BOOKS
NEW YORK

PRINTED IN THE UNITED STATES OF AMERICA
ON ACID-FREE PAPER
BY HADDON CRAFTSMEN, BLOOMSBURG, PENNSYLVANIA

To Karen Alarie and single parents everywhere.
May love find you.
Even if you're not looking for it.

.

Chapter One

The unhealthy emotion Michelle Germaine avoided at all costs, even to the detriment of her health, was anger.

No matter that her stomach was probably a world-leading producer of acid, she couldn't indulge in acid-purging fury. Her body's unfortunate physiological response to anger had taken care of that.

That's why, as she sat at a stoplight watching lightning slice the October sky, she told herself she wasn't angry at being summoned to the principal's office in the middle of the work day.

She plucked her purse off the passenger seat, rummaged through it and popped an antacid tablet into her mouth.

Thunder rumbled, and she bit her lip so hard it hurt. At this very minute, her skittish clients could be changing their minds about making an offer on the house they'd been about to buy. Michelle tried very

1

hard to thrust away her worries about lost commissions, unpaid bills and single motherhood.

Instead, she thought about the monumental misunderstanding awaiting her.

The school secretary had woven a fantastic tale. Supposedly, Michelle's son had gotten into a rip-roaring fight with a classmate. Jason had been strangely distant lately, but historically he was a sweet-tempered boy. How could he have walloped another eleven-year-old when he'd previously only hit the baseballs opposing pitchers threw to him?

The light turned green, and Michelle pressed the sole of her soft suede shoe on the accelerator. Starlight Pond Middle School was just ahead on the right, and she could already spot the tall evergreens that shaded the grounds.

The sooner she exonerated her son, the sooner she could return to her jittery clients.

She switched on her turn signal with the flick of a long-nailed, pink-tipped finger. And immediately slammed on the brake. An oversized Jeep, traveling so swiftly it resembled a red blur, unexpectedly appeared from the opposite direction. Tires screeching, the Jeep zipped in front of her car into the school parking lot.

"What am I? Invisible?" she yelled. It didn't matter that the Jeep's driver couldn't possibly hear through her rolled-up car windows. She pressed down hard on the horn. One. Two. Three times. "This is not a phantomobile."

Lightning again tore through the sky, and this time the thunder followed closer after the flash. Nature's display reminded Michelle that she absolutely, positively could not lose her temper on the way to see the principal.

In and out. In and out. In and out.

She drew the air deeply into her lungs and slowly released it. Within moments, she had control of herself again.

She turned into the parking lot, determined to remain calm. She didn't even flinch when the red Jeep swung into a prime space just feet from the school's entrance. She had a glimpse of a tall man with thick, brown hair and a navy jersey-knit shirt emerging from the Jeep as she searched the small parking lot for another space.

The quest was pointless. Every space was filled. The infernal man in the Jeep had taken the last parking place, which meant she would have to park across the street in the shopping center lot. She simmered. This wouldn't have happened if *he* hadn't taken *her* parking space.

"If I ever get my hands on you . . ."

In and out. In and out. In and out.

She drew the calming air deeply into her lungs, but she still jerked the steering wheel as she exited the school grounds. Minutes later, she got out of the car and raised her eyes to the gray, menacing sky. Of course this would be the day she had remembered to take her umbrella into the real-estate office because of the threat of rain. And the day she had left it there.

She hadn't taken more than a half-dozen steps when the swollen clouds erupted, sending cool rain cascading over her. She made an ineffectual umbrella with her hands and tried to cover the hair she'd carefully blown dry and styled that morning. She quickened her pace, but oncoming traffic forced her to stop when she reached the highway.

Water had already collected on the road, and a van traveling too close to the curb sprayed it in Michelle's direction. She jumped back, but not quickly enough to miss getting splashed.

"See what you did!" she yelled, but her comment was directed at the dark-haired man who had stolen her parking space and banished her to the far-away lot. If it weren't for him, she'd already be inside the school. And she'd be dry.

Her carefully chosen linen suit was not only drenched, but dotted with mud. When she stepped off the curb directly into a puddle of water, she added her high-heeled suede shoes to the casualty list. Strands of shoulder-length blond hair hung wetly in her eyes, and she swiped at them.

Lightning again slashed through the gloom. She imagined a similar jagged bolt traveling inside her body, igniting the temper she fought so hard not to lose.

By the time she reached the entrance to the school, she knew it was no use. Any second now, like the sky, she was going to erupt.

The consequences be damned.

Chase Fletcher liked to kick back and relax whenever he could, even if it were only for a few minutes outside the closed door of a principal's office. He shifted his big body this way and that way in a wooden chair three sizes too small, and reluctantly gave up on relaxation. Very reluctantly.

He supposed it was just as well. He needed to use this time to figure out how to handle Lauren's latest transgression, and that subject wasn't conducive to relaxation.

The school secretary said his daughter had been in a fight, which Chase figured was probably at least half Lauren's fault. Hell, he wouldn't be surprised if Lauren were entirely to blame. She was the kind of kid who'd swing first and think later. He pitied the girl who'd been in the fight with her. Lauren would skip the hair pulling and go straight for the uppercut.

Chase typically didn't waste time on worrying, but now he felt his forehead furrow in an unfamiliar frown. Maybe he should start listening to his father's familiar refrain about finding Lauren a full-time mother. Maybe growing up as the only female in the three-person household which included his widowed father was giving the girl too many hard edges, edges a woman could smooth. Heaven knew Lauren didn't see her own mother often enough to even out the rough patches.

His thoughts drifted back decades to his own mother. He closed his eyes, and he could picture her. Pretty and pink-cheeked as she leaned over the kitchen stove, checking on the hamburger stroganoff that had been Chase's favorite. Wiping her hands on her apron as she turned and caught sight of him, her face creasing in a loving smile before she wrapped him in a spontaneous hug.

Chase had been eight when cancer claimed her,

which was old enough to know exactly how much he and his father were losing.

Lauren hadn't even had her mother in the house full time for that long. He and Andrea had divorced when the girl was barely two, and Lauren didn't remember living with her. Despite the expensive gifts Andrea routinely mailed across country every birthday and holiday and the visitation rights she exercised twice annually, Lauren didn't know her well enough to miss her.

He'd certainly never missed his ex-wife after she left, except for Lauren's sake, but now he wished he had somebody besides his father with whom to face the challenges of day-to-day life with a pre-teen. Somebody female who cared about Lauren as much as he did.

Somebody soft and warmhearted who cared about him, too.

A movement beside the secretary's vacant desk caught his eye, and he turned to see a female face so lovely that for a moment he thought God had answered his prayers. Then he noticed that everything that went with the face was woefully bedraggled.

The rain had darkened hair he'd wager was blond to ash brown, and not an inch of the woman was dry. Even her shoes made a squishing noise as she walked. Her rose-colored suit was sweetly feminine but hopelessly wrinkled and dotted with mud. It made her look like a wilted ladybug. The thought made him smile.

She was a mess, all right, but an extremely appealing mess. She had curves in all the right places, even if they weren't as generous as he usually preferred.

Her legs were proportionally long for her height, which was pixie size, just a couple of inches over five feet tall.

Heat shot through him, unexpected in its intensity, and the uncomfortable seat became even more so. He squirmed and then turned his attention back to her beautiful face, curious to see what color her eyes were.

For an instant, her eyes made him think of the deep, blue sea. Then he realized it was storming in the sea.

"You're the man in the Jeep!"

Her anger, for some unfathomable reason, was directed at him. Still, he couldn't resist teasing her. A corner of his mouth lifted. "Actually, I'm the man in the chair."

She advanced toward him, her steps quick and jerky, and stopped when she was barely a foot away. She smelled of a light, citrus perfume and rain water.

"You cut me off! And then you stole my parking place!"

He screwed up his forehead, because she wasn't making sense. Now that she was closer, he saw that something strange was going on with that enchanting face. "I'd like to have a conversation with you, sugar. I really would. But I don't know what you're talking about."

"Don't you dare call me sugar!"

He tilted his head as he regarded her. "It doesn't quite fit, does it? You don't seem very sweet. How about I call you crab apple?"

His remark rendered her speechless for a moment. He took the opportunity to study her, examining the heart shape of her face, the pouty pink of her lips and the slope of her pert nose. That was it. Her nose. There was something wrong with her nose.

"If you have hay fever, you can use my handkerchief," he offered.

"Don't change the subject!" she retorted, swiping at her quivering nose. "You deliberately cut me off! You probably knew how small the parking lot was!"

"Now wait there just a minute, crab apple." A strange rumbling reverberated inside him, and he thought it was something in addition to desire. If he didn't know better, he'd think his long-dormant temper was coming to life. "How could I have deliberately cut off anything of yours when I've never seen you before? I'm as innocent as a newborn baby."

"Innocent?" She laughed harshly. "Try reckless. I had to slam on my brakes so I wouldn't slam into you! Then you didn't even have the decency to let me have a parking space that was rightfully mine!"

Decency? This bedraggled pixie with the quivering nose was saying, mere moments after she'd first laid eyes on him, that he wasn't decent. Why, a more decent man than Chase Fletcher didn't exist! He opened doors for little old ladies, for pete's sake. He didn't pass a homeless person without giving up some change. He even went to church on Sundays.

He unfolded his long limbs from the chair, muscle by muscle, joint by joint, until he loomed over her. Then he gave her his best don't-mess-with-me glare, the one that had kept pitchers from brushing him off the plate in his baseball-playing days. Never mind that he never would have charged the mound.

"I'm all for women's rights, crab apple. So don't

think I'm going to do you any favors just because you're a pretty little thing."

Her blue eyes blazed up into his brown ones, and he wouldn't have admitted for a front-row seat at the World Series that he would have given up the parking space had he spotted her. Which he emphatically had not.

"Listen, you big bully." She took a step closer. Her breath, when it blasted him, was sweet. "I know all about men like you. You're no more a feminist than Jerry Falwell! Feminists don't call women pretty little things."

"I was trying to say something nice," he said through teeth that were, amazingly, clenched.

"Don't do me any favors." She glared up at him. "And don't think you can use the fact that you're seven feet tall as an intimidation tactic."

His temper, the one he never lost, flared like a lighted candle fortified with oxygen. When he spoke, it was in a soft voice he barely recognized as his own.

"I'm six feet four," he said. "And I'm not trying to intimidate you. I'm trying to bring up the possibility that you don't drive any better than Miss Daisy."

Whereas a moment ago, Chase's voice had been soft, now it was loud enough to rival the school's intercom system. It was so loud, in fact, that it obliterated the sound of the principal's door opening.

The pretty pixie's nose, which hadn't stopped quivering, entered hyper speed. Then she sneezed.

"What a foolish thing to say!" She sneezed again.

This time, Chase was the one who took a step toward her. She didn't retreat. She also didn't stop sneezing.

"Look who's talking!" he yelled. "A woman who doesn't know enough not to go out in the rain without an umbrella!"

"I'm not sneezing because I'm catching cold," she said, sneezing. If watery eyes could catch fire, hers would have. "I sneeze when I get angry, and you made me angry. I wouldn't even have needed an umbrella if it weren't for you. You . . . you . . . big jerk." Sneeze.

"Sounds to me like the pot's calling the kettle black," he shot back.

"At least I'm not a lout!" Sneeze.

"Oh, no? Says who?"

Three loud hand claps stopped the barrage of insults, but neither of them turned in the direction of the sound. They were too busy trying to wither each other with nasty looks. Michelle might have won the staredown if her sneezes hadn't ruined the menacing effect.

"Mr. Fletcher! Ms. Germaine!"

The booming voice demanded attention. They turned in unison toward a thin, well-dressed man, his mouth a slash across his face. His hands were crossed over his chest in the age-old sign of disapproval. Even under the wire-framed glasses perched on his nose, his stare could have wilted a flower in full bloom.

Flanking him were a tall, chestnut-haired boy and a leggy girl with dark hair pulled back in a disheveled ponytail. They were covered, from the tops of their heads to their tennis shoes, in streaks of paint in every shade of the rainbow.

The girl had green-and-red stripes in her hair and all over her blue-jean overalls. The boy's face had taken the brunt of the damage. It was marred with black and yellow smears, as though somebody had done a poor job of applying war paint.

"Mom?" The boy addressed the wilted ladybug, who promptly sneezed again.

"Dad?" The girl asked of the scowling man who never lost his temper.

"I must say that was the most childish display I have ever witnessed in all the years I've been teaching. If you two aren't thoroughly ashamed of yourselves, I dare say you should be."

Thurman Goodman, wearing a striped bow tie and his best scowl of disapproval, sat behind the oak desk in the principal's office and leveled harsh looks in turn at Michelle and the man he'd referred to as Mr. Fletcher. Their paint-speckled children had been entrusted to the stern-faced care of the office manager so the adults could speak in privacy.

"What do you have to say for yourselves?"

Michelle stole a glance at her partner in crime. He was looking directly at her, and it piqued her that he was looking good. She guessed he was in his mid-thirties, and he had a careless, tousled look about him that was aggravatingly attractive.

His nose was a bit long but it was the perfect fit for his face, and his chin came to a strong point just below his generous mouth. His hair was the color of the dining-room set she coveted but couldn't afford: a rich, lustrous mahogany. She wasn't even going to let herself think about his body.

She looked quickly away, but took with her an impression of his eyes. They were very attractive eyes. Chocolate brown with a decided twinkle in them.

"We'll see that it doesn't happen again, sir," he said, and it sounded like his best imitation of a contrite little boy.

Michelle suppressed a smile. Her anger, as it always did, had fizzled as swiftly as it had materialized. But that didn't mean she had forgiven him. So he was handsome. So he had a sense of humor. He was also infuriating and responsible for the verbal lashing she was taking.

"Does that go for you, too, Ms. Germaine?"

"Believe me, I don't usually act that way." Michelle couldn't bring herself to make any promises about something that wasn't her fault, so she bestowed Mr. Goodman with her brightest smile. She wiped at her still-watering nose with the tissue he had given her, and he returned her smile.

"I'm quite aware of that, Ms. Germaine. I can still taste those delicious chocolate-chip cookies you baked for the PTA fund-raising drive. They were mouth watering."

"I have to confess that I didn't bake them. They were store bought," Michelle said, thinking that despite his bark Mr. Goodman really was a lovely man. She'd met him before, because he was Jason's sixth-grade homeroom teacher. He wasn't much older than she was, probably in his late thirties. He was doing double duty as interim principal, but that would only last as long as the genuine article was on maternity leave.

"But still delicious." He smiled again, and the good-looking troublemaker with the Jeep cleared his throat.

"Excuse me," he said in that unhurried way he had of speaking. "I'm sure the bakery made tasty cookies, but we were talking about how dreadfully Ms. Germaine behaved outside your office."

"How dreadfully I behaved?" Michelle's mouth dropped open as she turned her attention to him. "What about you?"

"I've already apologized." He raised eyebrows that were a beautiful shape and thickness. "You didn't."

"You didn't apologize! You just said it wouldn't happen again!" Michelle felt the first tingling inside her nose and immediately covered it with the tissue.

"That's more than you said!"

"Mr. Fletcher! Ms. Germaine! Stop that this instant." Mr. Goodman's voice was strident. "I must say this is unprecedented. I called you here to talk about your children, not to mediate your arguments. If you don't stop immediately, I'll have to add a few miles to my daily run just to alleviate the stress of dealing with you."

Michelle slumped back in her chair and crossed her arms over her chest. "He started it," she muttered under her breath.

"You two obviously have a prior relationship that has left some hard feelings," Mr. Goodman said, "but you should put it aside for the good of your children."

"We don't have a prior relationship," Michelle denied hotly. "We haven't even officially met."

"Chase Fletcher," the troublemaker said, extending a hand. She pretended not to see it, which was difficult considering it was so large he could have palmed the globe of the world sitting on the corner of the principal's desk.

When he didn't let the hand drop, she rolled her eyes. If she didn't willingly touch him, she'd appear rude. Or, even worse, cowardly. She reluctantly reached out. His hand was warm and firm. And electrifying.

"Michelle Germaine," she said before she pulled her hand from his. Great. The first jolt of sexual attraction she'd felt in eons had been caused by a man who infuriated her.

Worse, he had a name that somehow conjured erotic thoughts. *Chase*. It made her think of a chaise lounge with a seat long enough for outstretched legs. It made her wonder just how accommodating that chaise lounge would be for two people intent on enjoying each other.

As though she could ever enjoy somebody as maddening as Chase Fletcher.

"What did you mean about our children, Mr. Goodman?" Michelle asked, determined to get her mind off Chase and his electrifying touch. She thought of Jason and the pretty young girl who looked so much like her father. "Why did they have paint all over them?"

"I don't know if you're aware of this," Mr. Goodman said, putting his elbows on the desk and leaning forward, "but Lauren and Jason have had a problem since the first day of school."

"What kind of a problem?" Chase asked.

"They clash." Mr. Goodman pursed his lips. "They're like oil and water. I've already made sure their desks are across the room, because they can't seem to be around each other without arguing and shouting."

"Arguing and shouting? That doesn't sound like Jason."

"Jason is usually not a problem, Ms. Germaine—"

"Please call me Michelle," she interrupted.

"Michelle," Mr. Goodman said, smiling briefly before his countenance settled into its more typical serious lines. "But all bets are off when it comes to his relationship with Mr. Fletcher's daughter. Despite my best efforts, their animosity has been escalating. Today, it culminated in a rather ugly display of paint throwing."

"So you're saying they were flinging paint at each other?" Chase asked.

"Exactly," Mr. Goodman answered. "I don't know what precipitated the attack, but the aftermath was rather ugly. They're cleaning up the paint right now. When they're through, I'm suspending them for the rest of the day."

Michelle's eyes grew wide and horrified, although she should have figured out the reason for the children's paint-splattered appearance before this point. Even now, it was hard to twist her mind to imagine Jason hurling tubs of paint at that pretty young girl. She thought of Jason's name-brand jeans and athletic shoes, bought on deep discount during a sale, and cringed. They were ruined.

"But why would Jason do something like that?" she

asked, her mind frantically trying to make sense of it all. Her son never got into fights. He certainly didn't get into fights with girls. "Did Lauren provoke him?"

"Oh, come on," Chase said. "Lauren's no angel, but I saw two kids with paint all over them. And only one of them was mine."

"I'm simply trying to get to the bottom of this."

"I'm all for that, but if your son's anything like you, I doubt he's blameless in this whole paint-throwing matter."

"If I had a tub of paint in my hands right now, you'd do well to duck!" Michelle said, and he put out his hand with his palm up.

"I rest my case."

"Why, you . . ." A sneeze interrupted what Michelle had been about to say.

"Stop this right now!" Mr. Goodman said. "The two of you are worse than your children. We're not going to get anything accomplished if you keep this up."

Michelle lowered her eyes and took deep, calming breaths while she dabbed at her nose. *In and out. In and out. In and out.* When she raised her eyes to Mr. Goodman's, her olfactory nerves were working. Since she'd stopped sneezing, she could actually smell again. Unfortunately, the whiff she got was of a heavenly outdoorsy scent that could only be coming from the man seated next to her. It figured. Not only was he attractive, but he had to smell good, too.

"I'm sorry, Mr. Goodman," Michelle said. "As I said before, I don't usually act this way."

"I know you don't, dear," Mr. Goodman said. Chase made a noise, and Michelle turned in time to see him rolling his eyes. She ignored him. "Considering my profession, I realize better than most that all of us have a bad day every now and again. It even happens to me. That's why I run thirty miles a week. To keep my body healthy and my mind clear. I recommend it highly for both of you. Why, just this morning I was upset because I'd gotten a stone in my running shoe and—"

"What did you want to get accomplished, Mr. Goodman?" Chase interrupted. The principal looked at him blankly for a minute and then blinked.

"We're not going to get anything accomplished unless the two of you hear me out without lashing out at each other," the principal said sternly. "Do you think you can do that?"

Michelle nodded. She assumed that Chase did the same, but she didn't know for sure because she wasn't looking at him. The problem was that her traitorous eyes wanted to look at him.

"I'd like each of you to have a talk with your children on the importance of getting along with others." Mr. Goodman paused and frowned, looking from Chase to Michelle. "Maybe I should get something straight first. You both do believe it's important to get along with others, don't you?"

"Of course I believe that," Michelle said.

"Who am I to argue with the lady," Chase said, and the answer seemed to satisfy Mr. Goodman. Michelle, however, thought Chase had managed to convey he didn't believe her without saying what he believed himself.

She wondered how his wife tolerated him. Of

course, any sanity-preserving wife would have run from him as fast as her feet would travel. She peeked at the ring finger of Chase's left hand, and saw it was bare. Relief washed over her like the rain shower that had drenched her outside the school.

Of course, she was only relieved because she didn't like to think of him enraging some poor, innocent female day after day. On the other hand, a lot of married men didn't wear wedding rings so that didn't mean . . .

"Michelle? Is that agreeable with you?"

Michelle tore her eyes away from Chase's hand, which was very nicely shaped for such a large hand. Mr. Goodman was looking at her expectantly, and Michelle didn't have a clue as to why. If she admitted that, however, Chase would certainly figure out that she had been staring at him. As infuriating as he was, he might even conclude that she'd been desiring him.

"Of course it's agreeable," she said, summoning a smile.

"It's settled then. The two of you will act in the capacity of class chaperons on the field trip. Of course, I expect you to keep a particularly close watch on your own children so they don't disrupt the class."

"The field trip?" Michelle asked weakly, wondering what she had gotten herself into. The rain that had soaked her clothes seemed to penetrate her skin, and she shivered.

"The field trip to the Museum of Scientific Marvels in Richmond." Chase slanted her a teasing look that somehow conveyed he knew exactly why she hadn't been listening.

Michelle ignored Chase's knowing eyes and turned

to Mr. Goodman while her stomach sank like a rock that had been pitched into a creek.

"You mean the *overnight* field trip? The one scheduled for this Friday?"

"That's what I just got through saying." Mr. Goodman answered like a teacher who didn't like to repeat himself. "The bus is leaving at six-thirty sharp, and we expect to be back at about ten Saturday morning."

This Friday. That was only two days off, not to mention one of the more popular days to show houses to prospective buyers. Michelle had a client scheduled for six o'clock Friday night and another for nine the following morning. She was so busy trying to stay afloat financially that she barely had time for regular meals, let alone a jaunt to a children's science museum.

"But I couldn't possibly—" she began, only to be interrupted by Chase.

"Mr. Goodman won't let Lauren and Jason go unless we come along."

Belatedly Michelle remembered signing a permission form for the upcoming field trip while her son chattered excitedly about it. Jason's favorite subject was science, and the museum had a hands-on learning center as well as an exhibit simulating an earthquake. The bottom line was that Michelle couldn't let her son miss this field trip.

"We're supposed to be the referees," Chase continued.

Michelle didn't know much about sports, but she knew referees were a little like the judges who banged gavels to keep order in the courtroom. Taking a gavel on the field trip would be a very bad idea. Before the end of the day, she might rap Chase upside the head with it.

"You need to keep in mind, however, that the referees never, ever yell at each other," Mr. Goodman said, and the deep worry lines radiating from his mouth suggested he was having second thoughts about his plan. "I must say that would set a very bad example for the children. Do you understand?"

"Don't worry, Mr. Goodman," Chase said. "I promise not to yell at Ms. Germaine unless she yells at me first."

It was another of his backhanded assurances, and it was on the tip of Michelle's tongue to tell him so. She would have, if she thought she could do it without yelling.

Since she doubted that, she pressed her lips together and directed her attention at Mr. Goodman. Then, with great difficulty, she managed to nod.

Chapter Two

"Hurry, Mom," Jason urged, desperation lacing his voice. "Hurry or we won't make it. The bus is leaving at six-thirty sharp."

Michelle barely eased up on the gas pedal as she jerked her Chevy into the school parking lot, but still the maneuver wasn't nearly as reckless as the one Chase Fletcher had pulled just days before.

Her stomach fluttered a little at the thought of seeing him again. Then she forcibly focused her attention on the bus idling at the curb, spewing exhaust fumes as visibly as Jason was spouting disappointment. Michelle heaved a sigh of relief that the bus hadn't left without them.

"See, Jason, you were worried for nothing." Michelle pulled the car into a space in the partially full lot and shut off the engine. "They're waiting for us. Even if they weren't, I'm sure we could have found the science museum on our own."

21

"The bus is leaving." Jason grabbed his backpack and yanked open the car door. He set off for the departing bus at a dead run, waving his arms like a runway worker at an airport.

"Hurry, Mom," Jason shouted over his shoulder, and Michelle released a heavy sigh. Her son was obviously past the point of reason.

She picked up her handbag, and locked the car. Her high-heeled shoes weren't made for running, but she hurried all the same. She didn't like to keep anyone waiting, even if only for ten minutes.

Ten minutes. That's what this was all about. She wished Jason understood those ten minutes had been an investment in their future. She had sacrificed her former job and her friends to move Jason into a better school district, which brought with it a higher cost of living. If she hadn't picked up the phone on the way out of the real-estate office, she wouldn't have a new client. And if she didn't solicit new clients, they couldn't afford to live in northern Virginia.

"And that's the way of the world," Michelle whispered aloud. "At least, that's the way of my world."

When she reached the bus, Michelle grabbed the silver railing leading to the interior and took a giant step. Riiiiiipppp. For a moment, she thought it was the sound of the fabric of her world tearing. Then she slowly lowered her eyes, and bit her lip so her mouth wouldn't gape open in dismay.

The slim skirt of her buttery yellow suit now had a side slit that extended well above mid thigh. She groaned. Clutching the material together and hoping her matching jacket concealed most of the damage, she climbed the rest of the way onto the bus.

"Thanks for waiting," she told the elderly, white-haired driver. He grunted. Thurman Goodman, sitting directly behind him, tapped the oversized face of a black rubber watch. The digital readout glowed in the encroaching twilight.

"I'm so sorry," Michelle said, but the principal's expression didn't lighten. Her eyes immediately dropped to his pockets, searching for a ruler he might use to rap her knuckles. "I got tied up at the office."

"I highly recommend you get one of these," he said in his best teacher's voice, still tapping the aggressively ugly watch. He rapped the back of the driver's seat. "We can go as soon as Ms. Germaine finds a seat."

Ms. Germaine? Michelle grimaced, thinking it was a bad sign that he'd reverted to formality. She scanned the bus for an empty space and immediately saw that finding one would be a problem. The bus was obviously transporting more than one class to the museum, and two people occupied every seat in sight.

Jason had found a space about a third of the way back next to a boy with hair no more than a quarter-inch long whose nickname was Perm. Jason told her he'd showed up the first day of school with a permanent. A barber had buzzed off his curls before the second day, but the nickname stuck.

Michelle pasted on a smile as she passed, but her son wouldn't meet her eyes. She kept smiling anyway, reminding herself that she had deliberately kept from him how much trouble she was having making the rent on their townhouse.

She lifted her chin, said hello to the perpetually perky president of the PTA whose name she couldn't remember and kept searching for the elusive empty seat. Her gaze zeroed in on Chase Fletcher like a homing pigeon even though he was near the back of the bus.

He stood out in the sea of adolescents, dark-haired, dark-eyed and with shoulders so broad they took up most of the seat back. She wondered if he felt as solid as he looked, and her mouth watered. She swallowed, disgusted with herself.

For two days, images of Chase had been running through her head, giving her the unwelcome feeling there was something missing in her life. Such as a man with whom she could share herself and her troubles.

But that was as naive as it was ridiculous. Her ex-husband had demonstrated that she couldn't rely on anyone but herself by leaving her alone and pregnant to pursue his dream of exploring Europe. She'd tried to track him down after Jason was born to claim child support, but it had been a hopeless quest. After a few years of trying, she had given up.

She'd proved over the last eleven years that she and Jason didn't need anyone but each other. She certainly didn't need a man. Least of all the infuriating one who was touching his fingers to his forehead in a brief salute. The sizzle of attraction turned instantly to annoyance, and Michelle had a childish urge to stick out her tongue.

Then it registered upon her that there was an empty

space beside him. *Please God,* she prayed fervently, *please don't let it be the only one.*

Chase watched the pretty pixie make her way down the aisle, not sure whether to congratulate or flog himself. Next to him was the only empty space on the bus, but it was still warm from the sixth-grade boy who'd been gleefully maintaining Spiderman was the coolest of the comic-book superheroes because he could hang upside down from a ceiling.

Chase had been about to put a vote in for Flash— with speed like his, the bad guys couldn't even catch him—when he'd glanced out the window and caught sight of Michelle rushing across the parking lot. She'd looked so lovely in the twilight, with her blond hair shimmering about her face like a halo, that he'd impulsively slid the Spiderman fan a dollar to move across the aisle.

Now she just looked annoyed, and that in turn made him remember how annoying she could be.

By the time she drew even with his seat, he thought a self-flogging was definitely in order. She'd been pretty when she was wet and bedraggled, but the dripdried Michelle was stunning. Dry, her hair was the color of buttercups. It complemented her pale skin and features so perfectly he knew that it was what nature, and not Clairol, had intended.

What Chase intended was not to let a beautiful, ambitious woman sidetrack him in his search for a mother for Lauren and a wife for himself. He hadn't been lying when he told Michelle he was in favor of equal rights but he knew some women counted homemaking as a career. He and Lauren needed somebody like that. Somebody soft and domestic who wanted to take care of the home front, maybe even make hamburger stroganoff. Somebody the opposite of his ex-wife and Michelle Germaine.

Besides, he wasn't entirely sure she was unmarried. She didn't wear a ring, but that didn't prove anything in this day and age. *Be polite*, he told himself. *Nobody could fault a man for being polite.*

"Hello, Michelle," he said, using his best manners and speaking loudly enough to be heard over the buzz of sixth-grade voices. The children sounded as excited as a busload of inmates released from prison for a day.

"Michelle?" She wrinkled her brow suspiciously. "You're actually going to call me by my given name?"

"I could come up with something else," he said, smiling easily. She was not going to lure him into an argument. Not this time. "But then you'd yell at me and Mr. Goodman would come back here and try to give us detention."

The bus lurched to life, and she staggered, clutching at the seat back before she went sprawling onto the floor. For a moment, she stood there, trying valiantly not to fall, while it occurred to Chase that she was avoiding the moment she'd have to sit down next to him.

As aggravating as that thought had the potential to be, he wouldn't let it get to him. He wouldn't let her get to him.

"Sit down anytime you like," he said, giving her another blithe smile. The bus came to an abrupt stop while the driver checked for traffic before pulling onto the main highway. The motion deposited her onto the seat with a thud.

She careened into him, but it wasn't the force of the collision that knocked his breath away. It was the soft, supple feel of her body against his, and a faint scent he thought was peaches. For a moment, just a moment, he let himself want. Then she jerked away from him.

"Sorry," she said, sliding to the edge of the seat.

"That's okay," he said. The wanting hadn't quite abated, so he added, "you can throw yourself at me any time you like."

"Does your wife know you say such outrageous things to other women?" she asked icily.

"If that's your way of asking if I'm married, the answer's no," he said, unsure of why he was baiting her. After all, he wanted to know whether she was single too. Not because he deemed her suitable wife material, but because he had a moral problem with wanting somebody else's wife. "How about you? Are you married?"

"That's none of your business," she retorted while temper danced from her eyes. And her wriggling nose. She covered the offending body part with her hand, a motion which drew her arm away from her thigh.

Chase blinked once. Then twice. Said thigh—perfectly shaped, heart-achingly luscious—was exposed nearly all the way to her hip. His fingers itched to reach out and touch the long, lovely length of leg to see if it were as soft as it looked. He clenched them into a fist.

"It's not polite to stare, Mr. Fletcher," she said, her hand dropping from her face so her voice sounded clearer—and frostier. He dragged his gaze away from her leg to look into her eyes and saw they were just as cold. Like chips of blue ice.

"Since we'll be spending the night together, you might as well call me Chase," he said. "And I wouldn't stare if you weren't exposing so much leg. That's a mighty short skirt."

"For your information, Mr. Fletcher," she said, drawing out his name so that the syllables stretched. "I tore my skirt getting on the bus. If you were a gentleman, you would have realized that and refrained from mentioning it."

"Now wait a minute," Chase protested. "If you were a lady, you wouldn't be calling my status as a gentleman into question."

"But I don't happen to believe there's any question that you aren't a gentleman!" she said. Her hand immediately snapped back up to her face, but not before Chase caught the beginnings of a nose quiver.

This time, Chase easily recognized the answering signs of his own temper flaring. That was because the last flare-up, his first in years, dated back to the last time he had seen Michelle Germaine. So he shut the mouth that wanted to yell at her, closed the eyes that were seeing red and mentally counted to five. When he opened his eyes again, he felt more in control.

"I'll let that go, because you don't know me well enough to make that kind of judgment," he said, proud of his restraint. "And because I don't feel like arguing the whole ninety minutes to Richmond."

"Ninety minutes," Michelle muttered. "We'll never make it that long without arguing."

"Maybe we would if we tried not talking," Chase said, and Michelle promptly shut up. He gazed out the window, vowing to keep from looking at the indecent amount of thigh that the rip in her skirt uncovered. But the panoramic countryside didn't compare with the view of the creamy smoothness of her thigh.

He imagined where that thigh led . . . and got an elbow in his side as she struggled out of her suit jacket and laid the garment over her leg. He refrained from telling her it was a sacrilege to cover something so beautiful, but just barely. The comment could very well get him an elbow in the mouth.

He kept his side of the bargain for the next fifteen minutes, even resting his eyes now that she'd covered the main reason he had to keep them open. The leg room was minimal, especially with Michelle sitting next to him, but he managed to make himself comfortable.

He could feel her fidgeting next to him, probably being extra careful not to touch him. He found the thought amusing, because it meant she was as aware of him as he was of her. The smell of peaches drifted into his nostrils, and he could feel himself drifting off.

"How can you sleep with all this noise around us?"

He opened one eye and peered at her. "I thought we weren't talking."

"I'm through being angry." She shrugged. "It's a cosmic flaw. I don't seem to be able to stay angry for more than a couple of minutes, not even at someone as maddening as you."

"Are you through being angry for the rest of the trip or for the moment?"

She seemed to ponder that. "For the moment, probably. But in the meantime, I thought maybe you could satisfy my curiosity."

"What do you want to know?" Chase asked, prepared for a barrage of personal questions. Instead she pointed to his daughter, the focus of attention of every girl within a two-seat radius.

"What does Lauren have that the other kids keep looking at?"

"Must be her autographed photo of 'NSync. My sister knows a friend of their manager's, so she was able to get one for her."

"What's 'NSync?"

He smiled. "You wouldn't ask if you had a daughter instead of a son. 'NSync's one of those boy bands. The girls go crazy over their music, and . . ." He indicated the group of girls straining to get a peek at Lauren's photo. ". . . the boys themselves."

"Oh."

She settled back in her seat, seemingly disinclined to say anything else. Her "oh" even sounded like a dismissal. For some reason, that irked him. Without thinking it through, he used the tagline sure to get a rise out of her.

"Does that satisfy your curiosity, sugar?"

Predictably, she shot him a huffy glance. "Didn't we already have a conversation about you not calling me sugar?"

"Sorry. I forgot," Chase said insincerely. He wasn't sure what it was about Michelle that made him want to tease her. "How about La Belle Michelle? You look as pretty as a princess going to a ball in that outfit.

What I've been wondering is how you're going to sleep in it."

"Sleep in it? Don't be silly. I brought a change of clothes," she retorted and then gasped aloud. She patted the empty strip of seat beside them and then leaned forward and felt the air beneath the seat.

"Lose something?" he asked casually. She turned panicked eyes to him, and the urge to tease her transformed into concern. "Look. If you did lose something, I'll help you find it."

"I didn't lose something. I forgot something," she moaned. "My backpack. With my sleeping bag and change of clothes. I left it in the trunk of my car. How could that have happened?"

"You were in a hurry because you thought you were going to miss the bus," he said, relaxing now that he knew her problem wasn't serious.

She took some deep breaths that didn't do anything to calm her. "You don't happen to know where we'll be sleeping, do you? I was hoping the museum had cots."

"Cots?" He laughed. "The only way a museum has cots is if the Egyptian mummies had been laid to rest on them. We're spending the night in sleeping bags, kiddo. On the floor."

"Oh, great."

"Mine is extra large," he said, eyes twinkling. "I'd be perfectly willing to share."

"Oh, you would, would you?" she shot back. "What makes you think I'd dream of taking you up on that offer?"

"Dream. Now there's an interesting choice of

words," Chase said, enjoying himself. "Because you do get a sort of dreamy look in your eyes when you look at me."

"Of all the foolish things to say," she hissed in a refrain that seemed familiar.

"Belle?" He cut her off before she managed to ignite his slow-to-burn temper.

"What?" she snapped, and every child within hearing range turned to look at them. Her nose twitched.

"I think we better go back to silence," he said. "We're not setting a good example for the children."

Michelle's panty hose itched, the waist band of her skirt cut into her stomach and her rip now extended farther up her thigh. It wasn't a good sign considering she'd be spending the night in her clothes.

At the moment, however, she had other worries. Such as how to avoid being trampled by a few thousand pounds of children heading for the exit of the bus and the entrance to the Museum of Scientific Marvels.

Chase was in front of her, because she'd insisted he precede her off the bus. There was no way she was going to walk ahead of him, wondering if he were ogling her. She watched him now, her eyes lingering on the way his blue jeans clung to his well-sculpted rear.

How God could have granted such stunning looks to such a maddening man was beyond her. She'd poked fun at his height when they first met, but he filled out every inch of it gloriously. His legs even looked muscular through the denim of his pants.

She'd only taken a few steps from the bus when he

turned abruptly, catching her eyes lingering on his rear end. She blushed furiously, but he grinned and called over his shoulder, "See you later, Belle."

Not if I see you first, Michelle thought darkly. Then she scowled, but the scowl was directed at herself. What was it about Chase Fletcher that made her forget everything she'd ever learned about acting like an adult? If he hadn't suggested they give each other the silent treatment, she would have staged a repeat of the scene outside the principal's office.

"Get a grip, Michelle," she muttered to herself as she moved along with the tide of sixth-graders. She quickened her pace, weaving in and out of the crowd, until she caught up to her son. He was a handsome boy, with smooth olive skin and a trendy haircut that left his hair long on top and short on the sides. She took in his baggy jeans and sweatshirt and was thankful at least one of them was dressed appropriately.

"Look at that giant pendulum, Jason," Michelle said, pointing to a massive gadget gently swinging to and fro as it hung suspended over the museum entrance. Even though Michelle knew it must impress him, he barely grunted in reply.

A trio of girls drew even with them, and the one closest to Michelle was Lauren Fletcher. She was wearing her long, dark hair down, and it swung as she walked. She regarded Michelle with liquid-brown eyes as big as a doe's as she fingered the chunky beads on her necklace.

"Hello, Ms. Germaine." She flashed Michelle a smile. "Nice to see you again. I didn't know your hair was so blond. It's really pretty."

"Why, thank you, Lauren," Michelle said, trying to figure out who had taught the girl such beautiful manners. It certainly couldn't have been her father. Lauren flashed the same charming smile at Jason.

"Hello, Jason."

"Cut it out, Lauren. You can't fool me. I know you're up to something," Jason tossed at her, giving her a sidelong glare.

"Jason!" Michelle sent a look of dismay at her son, but Lauren was impervious to the insult. She grinned wider and walked away with her friends.

"You don't know her like I do, Mom." Jason scuffed his feet as he walked. "She's planning something. I can feel it."

"I think you're being unfair. She seems like a perfectly nice girl."

"Don't defend her, Mom," Jason said. He increased his pace, leaving Michelle lagging behind.

"Ms. Germaine! Michelle! Could I have a word?"

Thurman Goodman's voice sounded from behind her, and Michelle gladly stopped, but not before she spotted Chase. The PTA president had fallen into step with him, and her round, pretty face filled with animated pleasure as she gazed up at him.

Michelle determinedly focused on Mr. Goodman. "How can I help you, Mr. Goodman?"

"Thurman," he said, and Michelle managed to smile. Dare she hope that she had been forgiven? "I need to tell you about tonight's scheduled activities and give you my spiel on field-trip rules. I gave the official briefing five minutes before the bus was supposed to leave. I must say that I wouldn't have to repeat it had you been on time."

"I'm sorry we were late," Michelle repeated, pitying the poor students who were late for his class.

As the principal relayed nuggets of ultra-sensible information, Michelle's gaze followed the PTA president and Chase.

He was laughing at something she said, and even from a distance she could tell his eyes crinkled charmingly at the corners. Chase put a hand on the other woman's shoulder, the same well-shaped hand that had jolted Michelle with sexual awareness.

By the time they entered the museum, Michelle had lost sight of the sexy troublemaker. The principal left her side to tell a noisy student that people were more likely to listen to a softly spoken word than a shout.

Michelle walked determinedly on, giving her name to a fresh-faced teenager wearing one of the "Overnight Marvel" T-shirts that clothed all of the museum staff.

"Open your eyes to the marvels around you," the teenager said as she checked Michelle's name off a list. Then she smiled. "You might as well, because we're not going to let you close them until about one in the morning."

As Michelle walked away, she heard the teenager repeat the same phrases to the group of youths behind her. Then a friendly voice with a pitch reminiscent of chalk squeaking on a blackboard assailed her ears.

"Michelle. It's so nice to see you again."

She turned to see the PTA president, sans Chase, beaming at her as though she were a long-lost friend.

Although she'd met her before, Michelle couldn't for the life of her remember the other woman's name. But that was why she'd once taken a course in word association. She pursed her lips. She was supposed to link a physical trait with a catch phrase to jar her memory.

That's it, she thought with satisfaction. The woman's voice was every bit as high-pitched as Snow White's had been in the animated classic.

"Hello, Snow," she said, smiling triumphantly. The other woman's brow furrowed.

"Snow?" She sounded puzzled. "Did you say Snow? My name's Dani. Dani White. Dani's short for Danielle. I'm Benny Joe's mother."

Michelle flushed crimson even as she processed the information about Dani being the mother of the boy nicknamed Perm. She opened her fashionable leather purse, pulled out the miniature bottle containing her antacid tablets and popped one.

"I'm sorry," she said as Dani squinted at her through curious eyes. "I'm not good at remembering names."

"Oh, that's okay. We're all good at something different. That's what makes the world go 'round."

Dani's smile was as guileless as her round, friendly face. A pert nose, ready smile and sprinkling of freckles complemented her large hazel eyes. Her short hair was wildly curly and she carried about ten pounds too many, but she would be called cute well into old age.

Chase Fletcher had certainly looked as though he found Dani White attractive as he'd strolled into the museum with her.

"I couldn't help noticing what you did to your skirt," Dani said, giving her a sympathetic smile.

Michelle frowned as she took in Dani's sensible attire. She was wearing tennis shoes, a jersey-knit shirt and denim jeans with an elasticized waist.

"I was going to stop home and change before the trip, but I got tied up at the office," Michelle said. "Then I left my change of clothes and sleeping bag in the trunk of the car."

"It won't be easy sleeping in that skirt, but I can help with the rest." Dani patted Michelle's arm consolingly. "I always bring an extra sleeping bag in case one of the kids forgets. It's yours if you want it. And, if you come into the restroom with me, I can fix that rip in your skirt right up."

"You can?" Michelle asked, hope flaring. It was replaced quickly by suspicion. "What are you, a fairy godmother?"

"No," Dani said, laughing, "I'm a mom with an awfully big purse and lots of supplies."

Her comment didn't make sense until they were inside the gleaming white restroom. Dani perched an oversized black bag on one of the sinks, rummaging through it until she pulled out a miniature sewing kit. "Voila!"

"You carry a sewing kit in your bag?" Michelle watched as Dani expertly threaded a needle with yellow thread.

"You never know when you'll need it," Dani said. "Now you sashay out of that skirt, and I'll fix it up in a jiff."

Michelle sashayed and then handed the garment to

Dani. As the other woman expertly pulled the needle in and out of the fabric, she watched her.

She wondered if Chase and Dani were dating, and the possibility was so unwelcome her stomach burned. Because of Dani, of course. She seemed too nice to get mixed up with the troublemaker.

"This is awfully nice of you, Dani," Michelle said lamely.

"Don't mention it. I'm just glad to have you along. For a while it looked like Thurman and me were going to be the only adults." Michelle wasn't yet used to calling the principal by his first name, so it took her a moment to realize that Dani was referring to Mr. Goodman. "It's tough to find parents willing to spend the night in a sleeping bag on the floor."

"Do you know the other chaperon well?" Michelle heard herself asking and bit her tongue. What had possessed her to come out with that?

"You mean Chase? I know him well enough to know he's a nice guy." She cut off the excess thread with miniature scissors and returned the skirt to Michelle. "There. All done."

"Thanks. You're a life saver," Michelle said as she wiggled back into her skirt. She raised a doubtful eyebrow at Dani, unwilling to drop the previous subject. "Nice isn't exactly the word I'd choose to describe Chase Fletcher."

"Okay, then. How about handsome? Charming? Well-mannered? And, most importantly, single. When you're a single mother like I am, you make it a point to know who's attached and who isn't." She smiled, as though just thinking about Chase gave her pleasure.

"Although I don't understand how anybody could have let him go. He's a real prize."

Michelle gaped at her. Was Dani talking about the same man who had cut her off in traffic, pronounced her a pretty little thing and implied she was a bad driver? The same man who had teased her on the bus?

Dani, seemingly oblivious to Michelle's bafflement, swung her enormous purse over her left shoulder and linked her right elbow with Michelle's.

"What do you say we go help out Chase and Thurman with our wild bunch?" she asked, smiling widely. "I'd wager that, about now, they're dying for reinforcements."

Michelle returned the smile, mostly because she couldn't help herself. It was going to be awfully hard to dislike Dani White. She didn't bother to figure out why she wanted to.

Chapter Three

A fifteen-foot-tall Tyrannosaurus Rex, its monstrous teeth bared, rose up on hind legs in preparation for an attack on a much smaller Maiasaura. The gloom of prehistoric twilight swirled around the mammoth beasts while the unearthly cries of other dinosaurs reverberated in the air. The T-Rex moved menacingly toward the smaller animal.

All around Chase, sixth-graders from Starlight Pond and the half-dozen other schools taking part in the overnighter raced through the traveling exhibit on the way to something more interesting. Chase thought the only way the T-Rex could get their attention was by coming to life and chasing them. With one notable exception, the children had long ago ceased being impressed by mechanical dinosaurs.

He considered the attacking Tyrannosaur once more, and the emotion that surged through him was neither indifference nor awe. It was guilt.

40

He could too easily picture himself as the T-Rex and Michelle Germaine as the small, defenseless Maiasaura.

What had he been thinking on the bus when he'd teased her to the point of nose twitching? He should have been apologizing for losing his temper instead of adding to his transgressions.

It wasn't that she wasn't annoying, because she most definitely was that. But he was thirty-one years old, a bonafide adult who had stopped deliberately trying to get a rise out of a female a couple of decades before.

If he didn't watch himself, he'd stoop to tugging on her hair when she was turned the other way.

"Mr. Fletcher, can I have a word?"

He tore his eyes away from the unfortunate Maiasaura to see Thurman Goodman covering the ground between them with quick, efficient steps. He'd eschewed his usual suit and his usual bow tie for khakis and a rugby shirt.

Chase grimaced dramatically. "Oh, no. What did Lauren do now?"

"Nothing yet," Mr. Goodman said, adjusting his wire-rimmed glasses. "At least, nothing I'm aware of. I wanted to keep you apprised of the situation at school and ask if you've done your part at home."

"My part?"

"Yes. Your part." Chase was surprised to realize that the principal was just a few inches shorter and probably only a few years older than he was. He had thick, dark-blond hair and a face women probably found attractive. He thought of Michelle flirting with

Mr. Goodman in his office, of him stopping her on the way into the museum. "Did you talk to Lauren about the importance of getting along with Jason?"

"Oh, that. Yes, I did. I grounded her for a day." Chase regarded him warily as an unwelcome thought struck him. "What did they throw at each other this time? Pencils? Rulers?" He cringed. "Scissors?"

"No. Nothing like that." Mr. Goodman waved away the thought with the flick of his wrist. "But there might be another battle brewing. I was thinking about it on my daily five-mile run this morning. I get up at six o'clock every day to get it in. It clears my head, not to mention gets my heart pumping. Running does wonders for the resting pulse rate."

He pressed one of the buttons on his rubber watch and examined the digital readout with satisfaction. "Sixty-one beats a minute, according to my watch's built-in heart monitor. Before I started running, it was eighty."

"What were you thinking about on your run?" Chase asked.

"Oh, that." The principal seemed to pull himself back from someplace else. Running nirvana, maybe. "Somebody's been pelting Jason in class with tiny wads of paper. The kids today, they're much too savvy for spitballs. They've taken to launching itty-bitty paper missiles at a target just for the satisfaction of seeing the target flinch."

Chase's eyebrows rose. He'd yet to get Lauren to take up softball, but that didn't mean she didn't like to throw things. "And you think Lauren has been doing this?"

"She's the most logical culprit, but I can't prove it. Yet. It only happens when my back is turned. And Lauren doesn't give away a thing." He paused. "I must say your daughter has one of the most angelic faces in the sixth grade. She looks like a saint, she does."

"So what do you suggest?" Chase asked, hoping Mr. Goodman wouldn't recommend plastic surgery.

"Watch her like a hawk." He scanned the immediate vicinity, and his lips set in a disapproving line. "By the way, where are Lauren and the five other children you're in charge of supervising?"

Chase scanned the prehistoric forest of mechanical dinosaurs, but the only one of his charges he spotted was a child the others referred to as Dinosaur Boy. He was staring transfixed at one of the beasts. His shirt was imprinted with its image.

"The rest of them are, uh, around here, uh, somewhere," Chase said.

"I suggest that you find them," Mr. Goodman said, and Chase prepared himself to hear a lecture about the role of a class chaperon on a field trip. Instead, a tremendous roar that sounded off to their right diverted his attention. A laughing Dani White stood in the middle of a gaggle of girls who were bellowing back at a trio of Allosaurs.

"There's Dani. I mean, Mrs. White," Mr. Goodman said. "If you'll excuse me, I must have a word with her."

Chase turned back to the exhibit he'd been studying before Mr. Goodman's arrival, and the T-Rex emitted another mechanical roar. The engineers who had built the smaller dinosaur had managed to make it look frightened, which was logical considering it was being menaced by a big bully.

Much like Chase had menaced a woman more than a foot shorter and one hundred pounds lighter than he was.

He checked his watch. They had another half hour of free time until their Starlight Pond group was scheduled to gather in a darkened theater for a laser light show. That was plenty of time for Chase to drag Dinosaur Boy away from the exhibit, locate his other five charges and offer an apology to Michelle.

He walked away from the dinosaur exhibit and went in search of the pretty pixie who had managed to make him feel like a T-Rex.

Michelle's feet hurt, and there was a dull ache behind her eyes she feared would soon become a full-fledged headache. Since the children were occupied with a hair-raising experiment dealing with static electricity, she slipped away from the group and found a deserted corner of the museum.

She sat down on a bench built for two, slipped off her shoes and rubbed one of her feet. A few yards from her, a skeleton waited to mimic the action of whoever mounted the stationary bicycle across from it. It wouldn't be Michelle. Three-inch heels were meant neither for bike riding nor traipsing around a museum.

That wasn't to say she wasn't enjoying herself. She'd spent time with Jason; shook, rattled and rolled in a restaurant booth that simulated the trembling of an earthquake; explored the night sky in the planetarium; and managed to avoid Chase Fletcher.

"Mind if I join you?" The voice was low and so rich it seemed to have been dipped in chocolate.

Michelle stopped rubbing her foot and looked up, cursing herself because she hadn't seen Chase coming. She was struck again by how physically imposing he was. His legs were impossibly long, his stomach washboard-flat. His chest was so broad, his shoulders so defined, that he probably lifted weights.

"If I said I did mind, you'd probably sit down anyway to annoy me."

"Is that what you think I do?" he asked, dropping down beside her on the short bench seat. She automatically moved away, teetering so near the edge she was in danger of falling. "Try to annoy you?"

"I don't think you have to try. It's an innate ability you have."

For some reason, her flippant comment seemed to bother him. The corners of his wide, luscious mouth turned downward, and he rubbed his chin. She noticed it had a cleft in its exact center. Sitting down, there wasn't as great a disparity in their heights. His beautiful, dark eyes met hers.

"Then we must have been standing in the same line when God gave out the ability to aggravate."

"I suppose that's another way of saying *I* aggravate *you*."

"I suppose it is."

"Good," she said, satisfaction enriching her voice. "I would hate to think this was one-sided."

He laughed, and Michelle wasn't prepared for the

way the deep, rumbling sound reverberated inside her. It felt as though he and his laugh had gotten under her skin. She turned her head sharply to look at him and winced at the pain.

"What's wrong?" Chase asked, instantly alert.

"Nothing." Michelle shook her head as she issued the denial, which brought on a fresh wave of pain. She winced again.

"I can tell something's wrong, and we've already established I'm aggravating enough to keep asking you about it until you tell me what it is."

"It's only a headache," Michelle said. She didn't want to feel vulnerable around him, and that's exactly what her admission had made her.

His eyes narrowed. "Do you get them often?"

"Often enough," Michelle answered. She reached into her purse, withdrew an antacid tablet and swallowed it. "It's nothing. Just something I've learned to live with."

"What did you take?" he asked. Too late, Michelle realized her mistake. Popping antacid tablets was so habitual that she hadn't thought about the consequences when she'd taken one in front of him. Unlike Dani White, he wasn't too polite to ask her about it.

"It's no big deal. It was just an antacid tablet."

He set his lips. "No big deal? You have an upset stomach and a headache, and you say it isn't a big deal?"

"It's not."

"Those are classic signs of tension, Michelle. The headache feels like a band tightening around your skull, doesn't it?" Her eyes flickered away from his so he wouldn't realize he was right. He sighed. "Go on, turn your shoulders so your back is to me."

"Why?"

"Because I'm going to help you."

"I don't need your help."

"I'm going to give it to you anyway." He put his hands on her shoulders and turned her. He hadn't touched her since she'd accidentally careened into him on the bus, and it was another chance for Michelle to disprove the theory that his touch was something special.

But the same, electric jolt surged through her, and she wanted to scream at something. Possibly herself. Preferably him. Then his fingers massaged the tense muscles in her back and neck, and the scream died before it could be born.

"Just relax," he said, his voice soothing and so near her ear she felt his warm breath rustling her hair. The intoxicating outdoorsy scent that seemed to be part of him invaded her nostrils. "You're so tense. Your muscles are as taut as guitar strings. You shouldn't let yourself get this tense."

Judging by the liquid, melting sensation weighing down her limbs, she shouldn't let him touch her either. She could deal with her headache on her own, the way she always had. But then his fingers moved to her temples, and she couldn't have told him to stop even if the commission from a house sale hung in the balance.

He had magic fingers. Long, supple, magic fingers that would undoubtedly feel heavenly no matter which part of her body they were on. They moved back down to her shoulder blades that longed to be touched.

"So is it your job that's making you so tense?" he asked in a conversational tone, and she felt like an over-stimulated fool. Her nonsensical reaction to him was doubtlessly because it had been so long since she'd allowed herself to enjoy physical contact with a man. It had nothing to do with Chase Fletcher himself.

"What if I said it was you?" Michelle answered, pleased that her voice didn't sound as breathless as she felt. He was on the wrong track about her job, which she loved despite drawbacks such as the clients who'd changed their minds about putting a bid on a house while she'd been yelling at him in the principal's office. It was her precarious financial situation that had tied her muscles in knots.

"I wouldn't believe you," he said easily. "I didn't make you late for the bus. Even a big jerk like me could see you came straight from work."

Michelle winced as she remembered herself hurling that insult at him outside Thurman Goodman's office. "That wasn't a very nice thing to say, was it?"

"No, it wasn't. But we're even, because I said some things that were equally rotten," he answered, that deep voice sending shivers scuttling up her arms. "I better watch out in the future or your husband's going to pop me one."

"I don't have a husband," she murmured, and Chase released the breath he'd been holding. "And don't you dare make a crack about how that's understandable."

"Why don't you have a husband?" he asked instead.

"Normally, I'd tell you that was none of your business. But, since you seem to know your tension-relieving business, I'll tell you the truth." She paused, and he thought he heard a purr of contentment as his thumbs kneaded the area between her shoulder blades. "I had a husband once. A long time ago. I don't want another, because I can function perfectly fine without one."

"Yeah, but when you have a child, it's easier to have someone to rely on."

"Wrong. When you have a child, your most important job is to protect that child. You can't let people into his life who won't be there for him when he needs them."

"Are you speaking from experience?"

"Yes. And in my experience, not all men are reliable, and most are more trouble than they're worth."

"That's not the smartest comment to make to a man who has his hands around your neck," he said dryly, and she laughed. A vibrant, throaty laugh at odds with her delicate appearance.

"If you think it's so great to have somebody to rely on, why don't you have a wife?"

The ends of her blond hair tickled Chase's hands as he massaged her slim shoulders, and he thought she smelled as fresh as a spring day. He could feel her muscles relaxing and thought it was in direct proportion to the tension building inside him.

"Believe me, I'm looking," he said, suddenly determined to make her understand that under no circumstances was he looking in her direction. Even if he wanted to turn her around and kiss her. "I learned from my previous mistake, so this time around I want a woman who'd rather have a family than a career. Somebody who'd be happy staying at home cooking, cleaning and baking."

"That comment reeks of male chauvinism."

"I didn't say I wanted a woman to give up her career for me. I said I wanted a woman who *wants* to make family her career. It would be her choice. Not mine."

"Except you would reap all the benefits. Some women actually get satisfaction from their work."

"Like you?" He was still fighting the temptation to kiss her, and his voice sounded hoarse. So he cleared his throat. "Tell me, what exactly is it that you do?"

"I'm a real estate agent."

"Ah," Chase said. "That explains why you're so tense."

"Tension goes with the territory when you don't get paid unless you make a sale. But that's also why real estate is exciting. Besides, pressure comes with most jobs."

"Not mine," Chase said, kneading her back a little more vigorously. "I'm a landscape architect. We surround ourselves with plants, lush greenery and flowers. It soothes the soul."

"Some of us have souls too restless to allow themselves to be soothed."

"Let me guess," Chase said, wanting his guess to be wrong. "You work all the time. Days, nights, weekends."

"In order to be successful, I have to," Michelle said, and then she swore softly. She reached around her body to her waist, and pulled a pager off a clip. As she checked the phone number, Chase saw that the pager was the kind that vibrated when a message was incoming.

"It's business," she said, as though there was nothing unusual about a client summoning her so late at night.

Disappointment radiated through him, and his fingers stilled on her shoulders. She was so driven to succeed in business that everything else that should have been important paled in comparison. She probably worked sixty hours a week, dropped her kid at day care at six o'clock in the morning and didn't pick him up until eight at night.

At the same time, Chase was miffed at himself for being disappointed. He, of all people, should have been able to recognize the type of woman she was. And he had seen through her, he reminded himself. That is, before he'd let his hormones get out of whack.

"If you'll excuse me, I have to make a phone call," she said, digging into her purse and pulling out a cellular phone.

"There are more important things in life than climbing the ladder of success," he said dryly.

"Not from where I'm standing, there's not," she said, and he withdrew his hands from her and inched away. The hell of it was that, even after having his worst suspicions confirmed, he wanted to move toward her. The heat that enveloped him when she was near was too powerful, too seductive to ignore.

She was about to say something else when he heard his name being called from a distance. Chase turned toward the sound and belatedly noticed that they were no longer alone in this corner of the museum.

Starlight Pond sixth-graders were everywhere, which meant they had finished their experiment and that he had once more fallen short in his duties as a chaperon.

"Mr. Fletcher! Mr. Fletcher!"

The voice grew nearer, and Chase saw that it belonged to Perm. The boy was out of breath when he drew even with the bench where Chase and Michelle sat, the color on his cheeks was high.

"Mr. Fletcher! Come quick!"

Chase's chest tightened as panic seized him. Oh, no. Lauren! What had happened to Lauren? "Is Lauren hurt?"

"No, sir," Perm said, gulping air, "but she's gonna hurt somebody if you don't come quick. Fists are gonna fly any second now. You better come. Pronto."

Oh great, Chase thought as he started to breathe normally again. Lauren was transforming into the female version of Muhammad Ali before his eyes. The girl needed a full-time mother—and fast. Perm bounced on the balls of his feet, anxious to get back to the scene of the action. Chase rose.

"You better come, too, Ms. Germaine," Perm said, almost as though it were an afterthought. "It's Jason she's fixing to sock."

They found Lauren and Jason in a corridor not far from the roaring dinosaurs, a crowd of children surrounding them. Behind them was an exhibit featuring a dozen miniature fountains that spouted in succession.

Even from a distance, Michelle could hear Lauren's voice raised in anger.

"You're a loathsome, beastly boy!" she shouted, shocking Michelle. She'd never heard her son described in such unflattering terms.

Michelle cast a quick look around, relieved Thurman Goodman was nowhere in sight. This kind of confrontation was exactly what she and Chase were supposed to prevent.

"Oh, yeah," Jason retorted just as loudly. "Well, I don't have my nose so far up in the air that all anyone can see are my nostrils."

Michelle was just tall enough to see past some of the other children to Jason's enraged face as she and Chase rushed toward the action. They were too late. Lauren advanced on Jason, her right arm cocked.

Michelle winced, expecting the girl to land an uppercut. Instead, Lauren plucked off Jason's Baltimore Orioles baseball cap and flung it into the water fountain. Then she smirked.

"You . . . you . . . !" Jason seemed paralyzed, but only for a moment. Then he moved forward, as menacingly as a jungle cat, and grabbed Lauren's necklace. He tugged, and beads fell to the floor in a pastel shower.

"You'll be sorry for that!" Lauren shouted, and this time she looked angry enough to strike him. The show, however, was over.

While Michelle had been paralyzed by horrified disbelief, Chase had pushed through the audience of sixth-graders. Now he stood between Lauren and

Jason. To Michelle, he looked like a towering angel of mercy.

"Children, stop this right now," Chase said in a deep, firm, no-nonsense voice.

"But she threw my hat in the fountain!" Jason wailed.

Lauren stuck her head around Chase's waist to glare at Jason. "You broke my favorite necklace!"

"Only 'cause you deserved it!"

"Jason, stop that!" Michelle, recovered from her temporary paralysis, rushed through the sea of children. She grasped her son by the shoulders. "You know better than to act like this. What's gotten into you?"

"What's gotten into me?" Jason was so outraged that his hands clenched into fists at his side. "Why don't you ask Laaaaauuuuren what's gotten into her?"

"I'll tell you what's gotten into me," Lauren yelled. "An annoying smart-aleck who thinks he's better than everybody else."

"Lauren, if you don't stop talking right now, I'm taking away your CD player for a week," Chase interrupted in a soft voice, and Lauren instantly quieted. Jason did not.

"I hope you never get to listen to another CD as long as you live," he shouted before pivoting and stalking away. Michelle watched him go as shock paralyzed her vocal cords. Never in Jason's eleven years had he acted like that.

Chase instructed his daughter to retrieve Jason's hat, and Lauren walked over to the fountain. Jason's hat was atop one of the spouting fountains, crazily tipping right, then left in the spray, and the girl waited for the water to subside. When she had retrieved the soggy cap, she handed it to Michelle.

"Here you go, Ms. Germaine," she mumbled, casting a wary eye at her father. Chase's expression was so daunting, it could have scared a living, breathing dinosaur. He moved closer to his daughter, speaking in a low voice, but Michelle still heard.

"Listen to me, young lady. I wasn't bluffing about your CD player. You stay away from Jason for the rest of this trip. Do you understand me?"

Lauren nodded, but she looked anything but apologetic. "Can I go now, sir?"

"Go. But remember, I won't be far behind."

Lauren took off, her strides long and angry. Michelle stared after her. "I wonder what she said to make Jason so angry," she murmured, half to herself.

Chase took a few steps to where she stood near the water exhibit. It was contained in a waist-high, twelve-foot square of a spongy material that had holes cut into it. A dozen gaily colored plastic balls rolled about the exhibit. Occasionally, like Jason's hat, one of the balls became suspended atop a water spout.

"What makes you think Lauren was the one who started it?" Chase asked.

"Because I've never seen Jason act like that before."

Chase put up a hand. "I'm not defending Lauren here, I'm really not. I know my daughter's more devil than angel."

"So you're thinking that Lauren started it, too?"

"No, I'm not. I'm trying to say that, if you'd spend

more time with Jason, you might notice your little angel has a devil of a temper."

Michelle's eyes narrowed. "What do you mean, if I'd spend more time with him?"

"C'mon, Michelle. You just got through telling me you work days, nights and weekends and that your job is the most important thing in your life."

Something rose in Michelle's breast, and she had a dreadful premonition that it was anger. The headache his magic fingers had soothed just moments before returned with a vengeance.

In and out. In and out. In and out.

She tried taking the calming breaths, but they didn't soothe her. She very much feared that, at this point, nothing would.

"How dare you imply that Jason isn't important to me," she said, her voice a controlled hiss.

Oops.

Mere minutes after apologizing for bringing her to the point of nose-quivering, Chase realized he'd done it again. He hadn't meant to. He'd merely wanted to point out that she'd handled the confrontation with her son all wrong.

"I wasn't doing that," he protested, and she sneezed.

"That's what it sounded like to me."

"No." Chase shook his head. He searched desperately for an explanation she would accept, but he already suspected nothing would make a difference. "I only meant that, if you spent more time with him, you might figure out Jason responds better to discipline than leniency."

She sneezed again, and she looked even more furious than his daughter had moments before. She came forward and poked him once in the chest.

"I was right before," she said and let out a succession of rapid-fire sneezes. "You really are a big jerk."

"Ms. Germaine!" Thurman Goodman's authoritative voice rang out from behind them. "Unhand that man immediately."

Michelle rolled her stormy blue eyes in obvious irritation. "Oh, relax," she said as she removed her finger from Chase's chest and whirled to face the principal. "I wasn't going to hit anybody, you know."

She must not have realized how close Mr. Goodman was, because her hand swept the air as she whirled and caught the edge of his wire-rimmed glasses, knocking them off his face.

The glasses fell to the floor . . . directly in the path of Dani White's foot.

Chapter Four

Michelle turned from one side to the other, desperately trying to find a spot on the unforgiving floor that would provide a smidgen of comfort. Her skirt twisted with her, bunching around her hips in a comfort-free tangle. She tugged at it, lifting her bottom off the floor and wriggling until the skirt was in a semblance of order.

Then she lay on her back and stared at the ceiling, directly into the only light illuminating this portion of the museum. She could feel the tile floor through Dani White's well-worn sleeping bag. It was obviously an old one, to be used only in emergencies, and she was grateful for it. She only wished it were fluffier, like the one in the trunk of her car.

She checked her watch, the face of which she could see perfectly even though it didn't glow in the dark. It was nearly three AM, hours after the rest of the group had fallen asleep.

She raised herself on an elbow and surveyed the sleeping people around her. Jason had camped out so far away from her that she could barely pick him out. It hurt that he'd done so deliberately, not setting down his bag until she'd already laid down hers.

She sighed. The teen years were ahead, and she wasn't sure she had the wisdom to get through them. How do you handle a rebellious child who was already taller than you were? Certainly not the way she'd handled him at the water fountain when he'd ripped off Lauren Fletcher's necklace.

As much as she hated to admit it, Chase had been right about one teensy aspect of her parenting. She wasn't much of a disciplinarian. That she'd never needed to be until lately didn't excuse her. She should have given Jason a talking to right then, the way Chase had done with Lauren.

She looked back over the room until she found Chase. Well, not found him, exactly. She'd been abundantly aware of him when they'd set up for the night, waiting for him to repeat his ridiculous invitation that she share his sleeping bag.

Instead, he'd barely glanced her way, and she'd told herself she was glad. She'd refused once. She would have refused again. She didn't want to be zipped inside his ridiculously large, outrageously downy sleeping bag with him, nestled against his warm, hard body, listening to his steady heartbeats and the soft cadence of his breathing.

Chase turned in his sleep so his face was toward her. One long arm was curled over his head, framing his tousled mahogany hair. Double fans of thick, dark eyelashes shaded his strong cheekbones. A faint shadow covered his jaw. His beautiful mouth was relaxed, making his lips look fuller, his mouth wider.

She stifled an overwhelming urge to get out of her thread-bare bag and crawl across the floor to him. When she got there, however, she wasn't sure whether she'd kiss him or wallop him for being able to sleep through this.

Michelle punched her pillow an instant before she realized she didn't have one. Her hand collided with the inflexible floor.

"Darnit," she yelped, then covered her mouth with her smarting hand. She took a quick, guilty look around to make sure she hadn't awakened anyone. The adolescent girl next to her tossed in her sleep, but didn't crack an eyelid.

Satisfied that all was peaceful, she sat up and quietly extracted herself from her sleeping bag. She debated for a moment whether to put on her shoes, then decided against it.

Thurman Goodman had made it crystal clear before they'd bedded down that wandering through the museum in the middle of the night wouldn't be tolerated. If the click of her heels awakened him, she'd be in even deeper trouble than she already was.

She crept away on her stockinged feet, intent on getting someplace where she could stretch her cramped limbs. Preferably someplace free of the temptation to turn and watch Chase Fletcher sleep and wonder what it would be like to be nestled close to the warm beauty of his slumberous body.

"Psssst, wait for me."

At the sound of the whispered voice, Michelle jumped and let out a loud gasp. Turning, she spied Chase, also without his shoes, following her across the museum floor.

"I thought you were asleep," she blurted out. He put his index finger to his lips.

"Shhhh. What are you trying to do? Wake up the principal? And how was I supposed to sleep when you were tossing and turning and, ah yes, yelping?"

"I slammed my hand on the floor when I noticed how you . . ." She stopped, realizing she couldn't tell him about her internal debate. "Oh, never mind," she said, forgetting to be quiet.

"Shhhh," he repeated. "Don't you know what the penalty is for playing hooky?" He lowered his voice dramatically. "Detention."

"But we're not—"

"Just be quiet. You don't want them to hear us, do you?" he whispered. Just to be contrary, she almost told him she didn't care who heard them. But that would be about as foolhardy as cavorting with him in the middle of the night. Sorry now that she hadn't put on her shoes to counteract the disparity in their heights, she tilted her head way back to tell him she was going back to sleep.

That was a mistake. He looked, simply, too fine. The first few buttons of his shirt had come undone, giving her a peek of beautifully developed pectoral muscles and fine, dark chest hair. A slight, sexy stubble covered his well-shaped chin, and his wide mouth was curved in a mischievous slant. His brown eyes were clear, and his dark hair so attractively mussed her stomach gave a tumble. Even his clothes were ridge free. Hers, she felt sure, were as wrinkled as a shar-pei's skin.

"Let's get out of here," he said, reaching out to take her hand. Annoyingly, his warm grasp dispelled the chill that had invaded her since she got out of the sleeping bag.

"But I don't—" she began.

"Shhhh," he admonished again. He walked away from the Starlight Pond group with his leisurely, hip-rolling walk, leading her by the hand. Even when he was in a hurry, she realized, he took his time. He didn't speak again until they were well away from the group. "Principal Goodman would have my hide if he saw me with you. He told me it was *imperative* for the success of the class field trip that I stay away from you."

He rounded a corner and headed into the darkness, down a wide corridor that headed she couldn't remember where.

"He told me the same thing," she confided as she followed him. "But I think he wants me to stay away from him, too."

He laughed, a rich sound that rumbled in the darkness and assaulted her senses. He stopped in front of what she thought was a door, but it was too dark to tell for sure. Their hands were still linked, and she didn't want to let go. She imagined them adrift in a sea of blackness where anything could happen.

"Should we?" he asked softly.

"Yes," she answered, although she wasn't sure what she was agreeing to. Did he want to know if she'd follow him deeper into an inky blackness that was filled with possibility? Was he asking for permission to kiss her, knowing that in the darkness only sensation mattered?

He flung open the door and shut it behind them. She waited in breathless anticipation to feel his mouth against hers. He moved, angling his body so that it was in front of hers. He bent at the waist, and his breath felt hot, so hot, on her skin. A tingling sensation shivered through her veins, warming her blood. She held her breath, waiting, waiting . . .

The lights flickered on, making her eyes smart. She blinked a few times while her pupils constricted, then focused on Chase. He was wearing a wide grin. He didn't look remotely like a man ready to feast on stolen kisses in the darkness. Disappointment flooded her. She deliberately stemmed the tide. Sure, kissing Chase Fletcher would have been enjoyable. It would also have been a colossal mistake.

"We're in the planetarium," she said flatly, stating the obvious. His dark eyes twinkled.

"What's the point of playing hooky if you're not going to take advantage of it?"

He didn't wait for an answer, but wove through an aisle until he reached the control panel in the middle of the room. He sat down in the same chair the operator had used earlier that evening. The Starlight Pond students had oohed and aahed as constellations flashed overhead while the room filled with the music of the Backstreet Boys.

"What are you doing now?" Michelle asked, shaking off the sensual haze she had no business letting engulf her and following the path he'd taken down the aisle. They were alone, but she was still whispering. He winked and gave her a conspiratorial grin, making her feel young again, like a schoolgirl who really was worried about being scolded by the principal.

"We'll skip the music, because it might wake everyone up," he said, studying the control panel in front of him. "Ah, here's what I want." He flipped a switch, plunging the room into darkness once again. Michelle stood perfectly still, wondering at the method to his madness.

"I give you," Chase said an instant before she heard the faint click of another switch, "the stars."

Streams of light projected from the control panel, filling the ceiling of the planetarium with the wonders of the heavens. Michelle's brain knew she was inside a science museum, but her heart soared free. Up, up into the simulated sky.

Stars winked at her from above, like diamonds sparkling on a rich bed of black velvet, looking impossibly beautiful. Her eyes teared. She couldn't remember the last time anyone had given her such a wonderful gift. She couldn't even recall the last time anyone had given her a gift.

She blinked back the tears as she got control of herself. She should thank him, but she couldn't. Not if she didn't want to look like a sentimental fool. "You were quoting from a science fiction book, weren't you?"

"You recognized it?"

She nodded. "It's from *The Stars My Destination*."

Chase's smile was wide and as dazzling as the stars

that twinkled above them. He hopped down from the control center, lowered himself into one of the seats that made a circular pattern around the room and tilted back his head. Instantly, he looked at ease.

"And so they are my destination," Chase replied, turning the book title into a double entendre. "Come sit next to me. Any woman who reads Alfred Bester can't be all bad. No matter what Principal Goodman says."

A smile tilted the corners of Michelle's mouth, and she used the light of the stars as she made her way across the room. She sat down beside him, and he gave her another grin that reached all the way to his brown eyes. Up this close, he looked better than the stars, but that wasn't what worried her.

This playful side of Chase Fletcher appealed to her, which was a dangerous revelation. She could handle the physical attraction as long as she kept in mind how much he annoyed her. If she let herself like him, not getting involved with him would be much more difficult.

And she couldn't get involved. Not with a man she couldn't trust to stick around any more than her ex-husband or the few boyfriends she hadn't realized Jason was attached to until they'd left. Chase was already on record as stating he was looking for the kind of woman she could never be. And she'd already learned the hard way that she and her son couldn't depend on anyone but each other.

His breath had a vaguely minty smell, like toothpaste. Her heartbeat quickened, and her palms grew damp. Darnit. Why did his lips have to look so kissable? And why did she keep forgetting how maddening he could be? If it weren't for him, she wouldn't be puzzling over how to stretch her budget for yet another expense.

"Mr. Goodman's holding me personally responsible for the replacement cost of his glasses," she told him, tilting her head back to look up at the stars.

"Forget about it." Chase's comment was instantaneous. "I'll buy him a new pair."

She looked from the stars back to Chase. Her back went ramrod straight. "You most certainly will not. It was my fault."

"But I was the one who made you angry."

"It's true that you provoked me," Michelle said, biting her lip, "but I shouldn't have lost my temper like that. Especially since you were right."

He blinked. "You're admitting I was right?"

"Not about everything." She didn't owe him an explanation, but she found herself giving him one. "You accused me of not spending any time with Jason, which couldn't be more wrong. When he's not in school, most likely he's with me."

"But you said you work all the time."

"And you, naturally, jumped to the wrong conclusion. I give open houses on weekends, sit in the office and wait for calls and show houses to clients. I do work a lot, but most of the time it's no problem if Jason's with me."

His eyes traveled over her face as he digested that, and she was annoyed to discover that his opinion of her mattered. After a moment, he said, "Then what did you mean when you said I was right?"

She sighed and leaned back against the seat's headrest, feasting her eyes on the stars, as though in them she might find the answers to her problems.

"I should have done something when he tore off Lauren's necklace. Anything would have been better than letting him walk away. Except I froze. I couldn't believe what I was seeing."

"I take it he doesn't usually give you much trouble."

"He doesn't usually give me *any* trouble," Michelle confirmed as she realized she'd never talked to anyone about this. It was her problem and hers alone. But maybe it wouldn't hurt to talk about it. Just this once. "We've been alone since the day he was born, so it's always been him and me against the world. You know, united we stand and all that. But in the last few months, he's turned into a stranger. It's like I don't even know him anymore."

"Tell me about it," Chase said. "Lauren's never been an easy child, but lately it's as though an impostor's inhabiting her body."

"Oh, I can't believe that," Michelle said. "I saw how you handled her today. Threatening to take away her CDs was perfect. You know exactly what makes her tick."

"Yeah, well, with Lauren that changes from day to day. The music thing's new. Don't get me wrong, I'm all for it. Before now, her number-one interest was pro wrestling. I tried to get my dad not to watch it when she was in the house, but it didn't do any good. Then he wonders why she slugs first and asks questions later."

"Your father lives with you?" Michelle asked.

She saw Chase nod out of the corner of her eye. "My mom died right about the time I got divorced. Having my dad around has been a godsend. Even though he does spend too much time with the Rock. I don't know how I could have raised Lauren without him."

"Where's her mother?"

Chase snorted. "Andrea's clear across the country in Los Angeles. She calls Lauren and sees her a couple times a year but she's more focused on her career than her child. If she wasn't, she never would have moved out there."

His bitterness startled her. She thought about his earlier comment about there being more important things in life than climbing the corporate ladder. No wonder he wanted to marry a woman who'd make family her career.

"What about you?" he asked. "You said you'd been married. What happened to Jason's father?"

Normally, Michelle told anyone who asked that it was none of their business. She didn't like admitting what a little fool she'd been back then, so willing to drop out of college just because a man wanted to marry her.

"We got divorced when I was nineteen," she heard herself say. "We were kids who made a mistake. I wanted to go back to college, and he wanted to see the world."

"Did you? Go back to college, I mean?"

She shook her head. "I found out I was pregnant, so I had to get a job. I tried to find Dennis, but he was off in Greece or some such place. After Jason was born, I kept on trying. I figured the least he owed Jason was child support."

"Did you ever find him?"

"Oh, yeah, I found him. I let him know he had a son, too," Michelle said. It had been a long time ago, but she still heard the lingering bitterness in her voice. "Turns out he wasn't much interested in being a father. Or in supporting his son. He's still over in Europe somewhere, much too far away to be concerned about court-ordered child support."

"Wow," Chase said. "How did you manage?"

"By learning that the only person I could rely upon was myself," she answered simply. It had been a difficult lesson, but a valuable one. As long as she remembered it, life couldn't hit her on the blind side.

"Didn't your parents help you?"

"I wasn't born until they were in their forties. They're retired now and living off social security. They have their own problems. They don't need to worry about mine."

Chase frowned. That wasn't the way things worked in his family. His father was so involved in his life and the lives of Chase's two sisters that their problems were his problems. Likewise, anything that concerned Chase's father concerned Chase. To his way of thinking, that's the way a family operated.

"Anyway, I don't need anyone's help," Michelle continued. She sounded as though relying on someone else was in the same category as, perhaps, theft. "I have a job I love. I can support myself *and* my son."

"But you said before that real estate was a pressure job, that you don't get paid if you don't make a sale,"

Chase interjected. "What's wrong with accepting a little help now and then?"

"I'll tell you what's wrong with it. It's false security. Relying on anyone besides yourself is not only foolhardy but irresponsible."

"Oh, come on. People rely on each other all the time."

"In your world, maybe. In mine, forget it."

"I take it this means you won't let me pay for Principal Goodman's glasses?"

"We've already been through this. It was my fault. I'm paying for the glasses."

Even though the room was in partial darkness, he could clearly see the determination in her eyes. Dammit. A couple hundred dollars would barely make a dimple in his checkbook. He feared it'd make a dent in Michelle's. When he'd cornered Dani White earlier that evening, she'd told him the Germaines were new to northern Virginia. That meant Michelle was building her real-estate contacts from scratch, a process that could seriously restrict cash flow.

"But it was at least half my fault," he argued. "I should pay half the cost."

"Half? Only half?"

"Yeah," he said, relieved when he heard the waver in her voice. She was actually buying his argument. "I wouldn't dream of paying your half. In fact, I refuse to pay your half."

She was silent for a long moment, obviously considering what he'd said. "I can live with that, considering I never would have knocked his glasses off if you didn't have a talent for being so maddening."

"That's me," he said, thinking that her face was even lovelier than the ceiling full of stars. It was heart shaped with a luscious pink bow of a mouth and those sea-blue eyes. "Call me Maddening Man. Long for madman. Which, I believe, is one of the names you called me when we first met."

She laughed, a hearty sound that both surprised and pleased him. With a laugh like that, she should laugh all the time. Instinctively, he knew that she didn't do so enough.

"I didn't call you a madman but I thought it," she said, "which only goes to prove that first impressions can, too, be right."

"Smart aleck," he said, chuckling.

She slanted him a smile from her pretty bow's mouth and then looked back up at the sparkling ceiling. Reluctantly, tearing his eyes away from her, he did the same. After a moment, the magic of the stars washed over him, the same way it had done so many times when he was a boy.

"I know there are supposed to be shapes in the sky, but for the life of me, I never could see it," Michelle said after a moment. "When I look up, all I see are stars."

"That's because you're not looking at it the right way," Chase said. "You know those connect-the-dots puzzles you do when you're a kid? Seeing shapes in the sky acts on the same principle. First, you have to know where to look. Then you mentally draw lines from one star to the next until something materializes."

"But how do you know where to look?"

"The easiest way is to locate the North Star and go

from there. You know the North Star's the brightest star in the sky, right?"

"Everyone knows that. That's it right there, isn't it?" Michelle asked, pointing.

"Yep. Now, look south until you find the Big Dipper. That's a series of seven bright stars that form a large scoop. Do you see that one?"

"Yes, but even I've found the Big Dipper before."

"I'll show you how the Big Dipper can turn into a bear." He leaned closer and inhaled the delicate scent of peaches. For an instant, he wondered if the peach was an aphrodisiac. Or what she'd do if he nuzzled her neck. He made himself focus on the sky. "Now imagine the handle of the dipper is a curve of a tail, and the scoop is part of a body. Can you see legs protruding from the scoop? The extension of the scoop becoming a head?"

"No. I told you I'm no good at these things."

"Then let me help you. Give me your pointer finger."

She narrowed her eyes, but did as he asked, pointing it at him as though aiming a gun.

"I said give me your finger," he said, amused. "Not shoot me with it."

"Oh, sorry," she said as he wrapped some of his fingers around hers. Her skin was soft and warm, making him want to feel more of it. He closed his eyes briefly, reminding himself that Michelle was nothing like the domestic goddess for whom he was searching. It didn't work.

"Okay now, let me guide you." He extended her arm and slowly traced the outline of the bear in the sky. "There's the head. Now the body and the legs. Now the tail."

"I see it," Michelle said excitedly after a minute, her breath warm on his face. His pulse tripped. "I actually see it."

"That's Ursa Major, the Great Bear," Chase said, without letting go of her. At this point, he wasn't sure that he could. "Legend has it that Jupiter caught sight of a beautiful huntress named Callisto and immediately desired her." He wondered briefly if Michelle's middle name was Callisto. "She bore him a son, Arcas, which infuriated Jupiter's wife, Juno. The jealous woman turned Callisto into a bear."

"But how did she end up in the sky?"

"There's more to the story," Chase said. "Can you find the Little Dipper? It's right beside the big one."

Again, he guided her finger through the outline of a Little Dipper. She swayed with him, perfectly in tune with his movements. He cleared his throat.

"That's Ursa Minor, the Lesser Bear. It's also Callisto's son Arcas."

"He's up there, too? Beside his mother for all eternity? Jason wouldn't stand for something like that. How'd they ever get Arcas to agree to it?"

"He didn't," Chase said, enjoying her sense of humor almost as much as her nearness. Who would have guessed La Belle Michelle was funny? "When Arcas was fifteen, he came across a bear when he was hunting in the forest. He was getting ready to shoot her when Jupiter intervened. To save Callisto, he transformed Arcas into a bear."

"Of course it wouldn't occur to him to transform Callisto back into a woman," she said dryly.

"Apparently not," Chase said, "because then he placed both mother and son in the heavens as neighboring constellations."

"How could he do that?"

Chase smiled. "In Roman mythology, he was king of the gods. He could do anything. In fact, Jupiter's in the sky himself."

"Where?"

"He's not so far away from Callisto."

"Convenient, huh?" Michelle said, sounding miffed. Chase chuckled.

"You haven't heard the half of it. According to myth, Taurus the bull is the form taken on by Jupiter when he became enamored of Princess Europa."

"Yet another woman?" Michelle asked.

"Yep. See him up there? Now use your imagination. The whole bull isn't up in the sky, only the head and shoulders."

Again, he guided her finger until they'd completed the outline of a bull. She'd edged nearer to him, and he could feel her soft, sweet breath on his cheek.

"I actually see him," Michelle said with heat. "The lout."

"Hey, don't shoot the messenger. I'm only relating the story."

"It was a great story," Michelle said.

He lowered their conjoined hands, but didn't drop hers. Instead, he turned it over and drew lazy circles on her palm with his index finger. Her insides melted.

"How do you know all this stuff?" she managed to ask.

"My mother. On summer nights, we used to sit in the backyard gazing up at the stars. She'd tell us stories about the constellations."

"Was she an astronomer?"

"Mom?" He seemed surprised that she'd asked the question. "Oh, no. Astronomy was just her hobby. She was, well, a mom. All she wanted was to stay at home and take care of us."

"Sort of like the woman you're looking for?"

"Exactly the kind of woman I'm looking for."

She turned her head, just a fraction, and their eyes met. They both knew he'd just described a woman who wasn't anything like Michelle, but it didn't seem to matter. For a moment, Michelle couldn't breathe. She could see herself reflected in his pupils. She looked wild, needy, hungry. All the things being this close to him made her feel.

Their faces were no more than six inches apart. They both moved, inexorably closer, splitting the distance between them until there was none. His lips moved over hers, hot and hungry, the way she'd always thought she didn't want to be kissed.

It was fiery. It was overwhelming. It was wonderful.

This wasn't just a kiss, she thought with amazement as she met his passion. This was a meeting of the minds, a conjoining of the souls. He cupped the back of her head, angling her mouth to give him greater access.

Her hands splayed in his thick, silky hair and her tongue circled his, making heat swirl through her. No man had ever made her feel this white-hot passion. No man had ever made her feel this . . . needy. And needy was something she couldn't afford to be. Pushing him away was the hardest thing she'd ever done. Next to meeting his wide, confused eyes.

"I'm not the woman you're looking for," she reminded him softly, "and I'm definitely not looking."

A shutter closed over his eyes, eradicating the passion. He rubbed a hand over his jaw. "You're right," he said.

A few minutes later, they walked back to their sleeping counterparts in silence, being careful not to touch. The distance between them had widened to a chasm.

"This'll be our little secret, Belle," he whispered before she returned to her sleeping bag. "But I think it would be best to forget it ever happened."

Michelle thought that would be for the best, too. But as she tossed on the cold, hard floor, being careful to keep her back to the spot where he lay, she realized forgetting would be impossible.

Chapter Five

With anger dictating her every movement, Michelle pulled her aging Chevy under a regulation-size basketball hoop in the driveway of a place she didn't want to be.

The house was small, no bigger than three bedrooms, with a one-car garage and a tiny porch that she could tell by sight opened into a split-level foyer. As far as houses in northern Virginia went, it was unremarkable. The yard was a different story.

The grass was so thick and lush, she imagined barefoot children running through it. Adding to the splendor were well-pruned trees whose leaves had begun to take on the oranges, reds and yellows of fall. Terraced flower boxes of chrysanthemums, their blooms yellow and maroon, lined one side of his house. Begonias and bushes with fiery red leaves surrounded the porch. The Garden of Eden probably hadn't looked so good.

At another time, she'd be tempted to knock on the

door to ask the name of the landscape architect who had designed it so she could recommend him to new home buyers.

But she already knew the architect's name, because this was Chase's house.

Never, never land. Where temptation was just a flight away and she could be fooled into believing that someone else would rescue her from the Captain Hooks of the world when she knew that she had to fight them alone.

Bracing her hands on the steering wheel, she turned to her son. "I can't believe we had to come over here."

Jason's jaw quivered, and his temples bulged. It seemed to Michelle that he was clenching his teeth. "We didn't have to," he muttered. It was the most he'd said in the past hour.

"Oh, no?" Michelle asked. "I suppose now you'll say that I should have ignored the fact that you had Lauren's 'NSync photo in your closet."

"You shouldn't have been looking in my closet," he said sullenly. "A guy should have some privacy."

"I was looking to see if you had another pair of blue jeans, Jason. You know, to replace the ones that don't fit anymore. And don't tell me you should have more privacy. Boys who steal need less privacy, not more."

Jason's brows shot up, and he looked his mother full in the face. He had big, blue eyes and a sprinkling of freckles across his nose that would have fooled Michelle into believing him innocent if she hadn't known better.

"I didn't steal Laaauuuren's stupid photo." He pronounced her name as though it were a dreaded disease. "I just took it for a while, because—"

"Taking something without permission is stealing, young man," Michelle interrupted, handing him the photo. "Now, come on. We might as well get this over with."

"Do I have to?" he whined. Michelle put a hand firmly on his back and nudged him closer to the car door.

"Yes, you have to," she said, feeling battle weary. This was the second time she and Jason had had it out that day. The first had been over her insistence that he come with her when she showed houses that evening and his contention that he was old enough to stay home alone. She'd won that argument, too. She didn't care that Jason was nearly a teenager. No way was she leaving him home alone at night.

They got out of the car, and Michelle motioned for Jason to precede her. She popped an antacid tablet on the sly as he walked up the fancy brick sidewalk, looking like he was headed for the guillotine. He took a backward glance at his mother when he reached the door. She crossed her hands over her chest. Shaking his head in disgust, he rang the doorbell.

"There's nobody home," he said no more than five seconds later, turning away from the door. He hadn't even taken a step when it opened. Jason's entire face fell. Michelle made a circular motion with her finger, signaling him to turn around.

"Can I help you?"

At the unfamiliar voice, Michelle edged forward, thinking they might have the wrong house. She came to a stop behind her son and knew immediately that they didn't.

Although he was about thirty pounds heavier than Chase, the man who'd asked the question was undoubtedly his father. He was tall and gray-haired, with thick brows, black-framed glasses and an open smile. Unlike Chase, Michelle liked him on sight. She nudged Jason. He gave her a long-suffering look before returning his attention to Chase's father.

"I'm Jason, and this is my mom Michelle Germaine," he said, sounding as though the words were being pulled from him. "Uh, is Lauren home?"

"Lauren? You're here to see Lauren?" Chase's father's smile encompassed them both, but he addressed Michelle. "And here I was hoping a pretty lady like you was here to see my son."

Michelle shook her head. She probably feared running into Chase even more than Jason did Lauren. Sitting in the dark sharing confidences with him had been far too intimate. Kissing him had felt far too good. Staying away from him was the only smart move. "You're Chase's father, aren't you?" she asked.

"Tom Fletcher, at your service," he said, holding out a hand. He shook hers, then Jason's, before clapping the boy on the back. "Come on in, and I'll round up that granddaughter of mine."

"You mean she's home?" Jason asked, groaning.

Tom's thick eyebrows rose. "You say that like you were hoping she wasn't."

"I was," Jason answered, and Tom laughed. His laugh sounded remarkably like Chase's. Deep, rumbling and heartfelt. But not nearly as sexy.

"I'll go get her anyway," he said as they came into the house. He looked at Michelle. "Chase isn't home from work yet."

"Hallelujah" was on the tip of Michelle's tongue, but she managed not to say it. Instead, she gave him a slight smile and walked into the family room, as Tom Fletcher indicated. Old newspapers, months' worth of sports magazines, used glasses and the stray dirty sock gave the room a lived-in look. If this was the state of the rest of the house, Michelle figured Chase was looking for a domestic goddess to clean it up.

The mess, of course, didn't bother Jason, who could make one of his own. He immediately headed for the fireplace mantle, on which sat a ball encased in glass and a framed photograph of a man in a baseball uniform.

"Wow," Jason said, looking closer at the man. "This is Mr. Fletcher. He must've played college ball for the University of Miami!"

"He was on scholarship there," Tom Fletcher said, reappearing. "He hit that ball out of the park to help his team win the College World Series when he was a junior. The boy could always put the bat on the ball."

"Cool!" Jason exclaimed. "Did he play pro ball?"

"Couldn't talk him into it." Chase's father shrugged. "He was drafted, but he said making the pros was too long a shot. He gave it all up to become an architect."

"That was probably wise," Michelle said at the same time her son rolled his eyes in disbelief. Tom Fletcher laughed.

"It's all a matter of perspective," he said. "Lauren'll

be down in a minute. I hope you'll stick around until Chase gets home, Michelle. He won't want to miss you."

"Oh, I don't know about that," Michelle said. Chase struck her as the kind of man who liked to take his time about things, but he'd sure gotten away from her in a hurry after their kiss.

"You *are* single, aren't you?" Tom asked, and Michelle smiled. Usually she would have been taken aback at the bluntness of the question, but Tom Fletcher managed to ask it without offending.

"Yes, I'm single."

"Good." He gave her a knowing smile. "Chase is single, too."

She was about to tell him she wasn't interested in his son, but thought better of it. The way she'd responded to Chase's kiss the other night, she doubted she'd sound convincing. Better to let Chase explain things to his father.

She looked over at her son, who'd resumed looking miserable as soon as Tom mentioned Lauren. Michelle almost felt sorry for him when Lauren appeared. Her hair was pulled back in a sloppy ponytail and her clothes looked like they were meant to be worn by a boy, but it didn't distract from how pretty she was. Neither did her appalled expression.

"Oh, gross. Jaaaaasoooon. What are you doing in my house? It's like something out of a nightmare," she wailed. Michelle took a step nearer her son, and Lauren's horrified expression cleared. Mostly. "Oh, hello, Ms. Germaine. I didn't see you there. That sure is a pretty suit you're wearing."

"Why, thank you, Lauren," Michelle said, smoothing the skirt of her powder-blue suit. It had soft lines and feminine flair, a combination she wouldn't have thought would appeal to Lauren. "Jason has something he wants to say to you."

Her son stuck out the 'NSync photo, his mouth set in a mutinous line. "Here," he said, which wasn't what Michelle had in mind.

"My 'NSync photo!" Lauren shrieked and snatched it out of his hand. "What are you doing with that?"

Jason didn't answer, fueling Lauren's outrage. "You took it when we were at the museum, didn't you? You took my photo."

"Now, Lauren, you don't know that happened," her grandfather cut in.

"Yes, I do," Lauren shouted. She advanced on Jason, poking him hard in the chest. "I ought to slug you, that's what I ought to do."

Lauren's color was high, her eyes blazing. Alarmed, Michelle stepped forward. The girl looked angry enough to do just what she said. Jason could probably withstand the blow. It's what he'd do in retaliation that worried Michelle.

"Jason's here to apologize, Lauren," Michelle said, putting a restraining hand on the girl's shoulder. "Aren't you, Jason?"

"Whatever," he said.

Michelle slanted him a warning look.

"Okay, I'm sorry," he said. "I shouldn't have taken your stupid photo."

"It is *not* stupid."

"Is too," Jason retorted. He gave a derisive snort.

"Not only can't the 'NSync boys sing, but they don't look good, either," he said, surprising Michelle. When she'd asked just the day before if her son knew of the group, he'd claimed to like it.

"Oh, no," Tom Fletcher mumbled, a comment that made sense an instant later.

"Why, I oughta . . ." Lauren sputtered. She cocked her arm, giving Michelle time to realize what she planned to do. She dragged the girl backward at the same time Lauren swung. The punch landed on air.

Jason took advantage of Lauren being off-balance to snatch the photo out of her other hand. "You stay away from me," he warned, holding up the photo, "or I'll rip this in half."

"What's going on here?"

Michelle swung her head around to see Chase enter the room, and her breath caught. He looked impossibly virile in an outdoorsman's working ensemble: khaki slacks, docksiders and a cream-colored shirt open at the first two buttons. His dark hair was disheveled, as though he couldn't bother to brush it. Lauren ran to him, flinging herself into his arms the way Michelle was tempted to. Until Lauren reminded her that their children were in the middle of a battle.

"It's that beastly Jason Germaine," she wailed. "He stole my 'NSync photo and now he's threatening to tear it in half. Make him give it back, Daddy."

"Now that you're here, Chase, I have a wrestling match on tape I've been meaning to watch," Tom Fletcher muttered, backing out of the room. Michelle wished she could go with him.

"Is that true, Jason?" Chase asked, fixing his dark

gaze on Jason. Michelle waited for her son to back down, but he kept holding the photo in front of him, his hands poised to tear it.

"Yeah, it's true." Jason's voice quavered. "But ask her what she did with my Mark McGwire rookie card."

"You have a Mark McGwire rookie card?" Chase's gruff voice lightened slightly. He sounded almost impressed.

"I had one," Jason corrected. "Lauren has it now."

Lauren had Jason's baseball card, the one he prized over all his possessions? That was news to Michelle. "Why didn't you tell me that?" she interjected.

Jason whirled on her. "You didn't give me a chance. You said you didn't want any argument from me. That we were coming over here no matter what I had to say about it."

With a sinking heart, Michelle realized she had said that. After the fiasco at the science museum, she'd vowed to be tougher when it came to disciplining her son. And she had been. Unfortunately, she would have handled the entire situation differently if she'd been aware of the extenuating circumstance.

Chase slanted her what looked like a commiserating glance, then turned to his daughter. "Lauren? Is what Jason said true? Did you take his baseball card?"

"Of course she did," Jason interjected, earning a malevolent glare from Lauren.

"I wouldn't have taken your stupid card if you hadn't thrown that paint on me," she shouted.

"You threw paint on me, too!"

Michelle's eyes widened in embarrassment and horror. This was inappropriate. This was unacceptable. She had to do something to stop it. She opened her mouth, but Chase beat her to it.

"Children, stop this right now," he ordered loudly. Even Michelle flinched. "I'll tell you what you're going to do. A trade. Jason's going to give Lauren back her photo, and Lauren's returning the Mark McGwire card."

"But—" Lauren began.

"No buts, young lady," Chase interrupted before Lauren could begin one of her famous circular arguments in which she was never to blame. "Lauren, go get the card right now."

He knew his daughter well enough to realize she wanted to refuse, but she was wilier than that. She wouldn't disobey a direct order. She whirled, her ponytail whipping the air. As soon as she was gone, Michelle turned to her son. "You should have told me she'd taken your card, Jason."

"You wouldn't have believed me," Jason shot back, and Chase watched the hurt come into Michelle's blue eyes. It stabbed at him, too. From their conversation in the planetarium, he knew Jason meant the world to her. By forcing Jason to return Lauren's photo, Michelle had only been trying to do the right thing.

"She's your mother. Of course she would have believed you." He moved closer to Michelle, wanting her to know he was on her side, wanting somehow to alleviate her pain. "Maybe if you'd trusted her, we could have avoided this whole scene."

He half expected Michelle to light into him for daring to help out with her son, but she still seemed dazed from Jason's verbal attack. Unable to stop himself, he put a hand out to touch her, and found her shoulder rigid with tension. He squeezed gently, massaging the tight muscles.

Jason's dark eyes took in Chase's gesture before they moved to his mother's pale face. He scuffed his feet on the carpet. "Well, maybe I should've," he conceded.

The tension in Michelle's shoulders lessened, but didn't abate. Chase barely resisted the urge to draw her into his arms and tell her everything would be okay. Which, in all honesty, was what he'd wanted to do since he came upon the staggering sight of her in his family room.

That wasn't all he wanted to do. Since their kiss, he hadn't been able to get her out of his mind. He'd even been thinking of her while walking up the sidewalk a few minutes ago.

He was imagining kissing her now, which wasn't the smartest move considering their audience of one was about to double. Loud stamps announced Lauren's return. She flung the baseball card at Jason, the angry effect ruined when it floated harmlessly to the floor. "Here's your lousy card," she yelled.

Not to be outdone, Jason threw the photo at her. It, too, drifted benignly until it settled on the carpet. "Here's your stupid photo."

Lauren snatched the photo off the floor and examined it for defects. Apparently finding none, she stomped out of the room without another word, maybe to join her grandfather in watching pro wrestling.

Chase thought her need for a greater female influence was never more evident.

"You should apologize to Mr. Fletcher for making a scene," Michelle said. Her voice was tight, but Chase wasn't sure whether it was from anger or embarrassment. His hand was still on her shoulder so he gave it a gentle squeeze, this time to communicate his support. She didn't even glance at him.

Jason looked from one parent to the next. His mouth twisted as he seemed to wrestle with himself. "I'm sorry about all this," he said finally, then turned entreating eyes to Chase, "but you should understand, Mr. Fletcher."

"I should?" That was news to him.

"You played baseball. You must've collected cards. The Mark McGwire rookie's my best one. I would've done anything to get it back." He held out the card. Chase could swear that the kid waggled his eyebrows. "Wanna see it?"

Of course Chase wanted to see it. It wasn't every day a kid came in the house with the rookie card of one of baseball's greatest sluggers. His hand fell from Michelle's shoulder. Unable to stop himself, Chase took the card and examined it closely. Sure enough, it was a Mark McGwire rookie card. Hot damn.

"Oh, for heaven's sake!" Michelle exclaimed, and Chase's head snapped up. She was glaring at him. All traces of the vulnerability she'd shown earlier were gone. It was as though somebody had poured vinegar back into the bottle.

"What'd I do?"

"The baseball thing," she answered, shaking her head. "You're doing the baseball-is-almighty thing."

Oh, that was all this was about. Chase shrugged his shoulders and grinned at her. "It is."

"All right!" Jason raised his palm and slapped Chase's. "Mom doesn't get it. She comes to my games, but she doesn't really understand. She doesn't know what it's like to have trouble at the plate."

"Are you having trouble at the plate?" Chase asked.

Jason rolled his eyes. "Am I ever. I'm two for the last twenty."

"There's a batting cage a couple miles from here. Want me to work on your swing with you?"

"I don't think—" Michelle began, but her son drowned out the rest of her words.

"Would you do that, Mr. Fletcher? Would you really?"

"Sure," Chase said, enjoying the boy's enthusiasm. "How about tomorrow at five? I can pick you up after I get off work."

"Cool," Jason exclaimed. They grinned at each other. It wasn't until Michelle spoke that Chase realized she wasn't smiling. Her eyes were narrowed, and the corners of her mouth pulled downward. What's more, her nose was quivering. Uh-oh.

"Jason, would you wait in the car?"

"Sure, Mom," Jason said, then grinned at Chase. "Just as soon as Mr. Fletcher gives me my card back."

"Here you go," Chase said, reluctantly handing it over. Jason bounded toward the door, looking back over his shoulder before he left the house. "See you tomorrow, Mr. Fletcher."

Chase didn't wait for Michelle to speak once they were alone, pretty sure she was spoiling for another argument. Her nose had tipped him off to that.

"I've got to hand it to you for the way you marched Jason over here today to right his wrong," he said, hoping a compliment would diffuse her inexplicable temper. "I was wrong to say you don't discipline him."

He tried his best smile to show he was sincere. She scowled back but still looked delectable, reminding him of why he'd lost his resolve not to touch her under the planetarium sky. If she hadn't broken off their kiss, he wouldn't have had the will to do it himself.

"I blamed him for something that was only half his fault," she pointed out.

"He was still to blame," Chase cut in, wanting to make her feel better. Raising a pre-teen was hard. He knew that first hand.

She took a deep, audible breath, clenched one small fist and sneezed. "Stop sticking up for me," she seethed. "I'm angry with you."

He'd known that. He just didn't know why. He was pretty sure he didn't want to know, but she looked hell bent on enlightening him. He shrugged and took the bait. "What'd I do now?"

"You made a promise to my son, that's what you did. How could you have?" Her lower lip trembled, as though she were truly upset. She wiped at her nose.

"Whoa there." He wanted to reach out and smooth the furrows from her brows but guessed she'd probably slap at his hand. "What's so terrible about making a promise?"

"First of all, you rewarded his bad behavior."

"He apologized—"

"Then you filled his head with empty promises. Do you realize he's going to be sitting by the door tomorrow waiting for you to come?"

"So what?" Chase said, still not understanding.

"Don't you realize how he'll feel when you don't show up?"

When he didn't show up? Chase ran a hand through his hair. Did she actually believe he'd break a promise to a child? His once-dormant temper, the one he hadn't lost since she'd set it off the last time, ignited. "But I am going to show up. I keep my promises."

"This one, maybe. But what about the next one?"

"If I say I'm going to do something," Chase said through clenched teeth, "I do it."

"Is that right?" Michelle somehow managed to convey that she didn't believe him. She advanced a step, until she was quivering nose to chest with him. In order for her glare to have its full effect, she had to tilt her head way back. "I'm not willing to take that chance. Remember that when you take Jason to the batting cage tomorrow. I don't want you making any more promises to my son."

She sneezed, pivoted and stalked to the door, her shapely rear moving nicely in the powder-blue suit. Chase watched her go, mentally reiterating the reasons he needed to stay away from her. Not only did she bristle far too easily, but she was as independent and career-minded as his ex-wife.

Even the way she was dressed illustrated her dedication to business. She wasn't going home to spend the evening with her family, the way he'd want his wife to. She was going out on business.

Despite all that, and the anger that still broiled inside his veins, he wanted her with every pore of his body.

"What'd you do?" The question came from his father, who ambled into the room to stand next to Chase and watch Michelle slam the door.

"To tell you the truth, Dad, with Michelle I'm never really sure."

"That's when you're in trouble, son," his father said, patting him consolingly on the arm. "That's when you're in trouble."

Chapter Six

Clutching the folder she'd forgotten in one hand and her briefcase in the other, Michelle kicked the door of her townhouse closed and rushed down the sidewalk to the communal parking lot.

If she hurried, she had just enough time to swing by Duncan Street to do a quick walk-through of a new listing before she was due to pick up Jason at a classmate's house. Barring traffic, she'd be back home before Chase swung by to get the boy for their date with the batting cage.

She'd cautioned Jason against expecting too much of the excursion, warning him that it was a one-time deal, but she'd gotten the sense he wasn't really listening.

She sighed. Her son didn't understand that the people who drifted into their lives would drift right back out again. He didn't yet know that the only way to protect yourself was not to let them get too close.

That she wanted to get way too close to Chase Fletcher both depressed and aggravated her. Maybe it was a natural reaction to keeping herself cloistered from romantic entanglements. After all, she couldn't remember the last time she had accepted a date.

Of course, she couldn't remember the last time she met a man who attracted her like Chase did. Quite possibly she never had. She wasn't only referring to his looks, although they were plenty appealing.

She liked the firm, gentle way he dealt with his daughter. Liked the calm air of lazy contentment that surrounded him. Liked the way he listened to her, as though he were really interested in what she had to say.

When he wasn't being aggravating, she just plain liked him.

Which was just plain dangerous. To herself as well as her son. Especially when he'd made it perfectly clear that he was searching for someone more along the lines of Betty Crocker than Gloria Steinem.

Trying to convince herself Chase's taste in women didn't matter, she raised her chin. And caught sight of the manager of the townhouse complex rushing toward her, which was just what she didn't need.

"Ms. Germaine, I'm glad I caught you," he said, puffing heavily to catch his breath. Dirk Brownley's short-sleeved dress shirt strained over his ample belly. A few long hairs from his combover dangled in his pasty face. "You didn't include your full rent payment in your envelope this month."

Michelle composed her features. This wasn't the first run-in she'd had with Dirk, who was about as understanding as Adolf Hitler. "I did include a note saying the rest of the payment would be late," she said. Better not to tell him she didn't have the rest of the payment yet. She'd figure that out later.

"You understand a late fee will be assessed on that amount." Dirk tapped his chin. "It would be better for all concerned if you'd get your payment in on time."

She smiled acidly. "I'll keep that in mind. Goodbye, Mr. Brownley."

"Goodbye, Ms. Germaine." He jerked a thumb at her car. "Too bad about your tire."

He walked away without another word, leaving Michelle to puzzle over what he meant. She didn't puzzle long. The rear tire on her once-serviceable sedan was as flat as the Sierra desert.

"This is just my luck," she said aloud, but caught herself before she indulged in feeling sorry for herself. She simply didn't have the time. "Okay. I can handle this." She snapped her fingers. "The *auto club* can handle this."

She was halfway back to her townhouse when a memory pierced her elation like a stuck balloon. The automobile renewal form had come in the mail last month, and she clearly remembered tossing it aside because other bills were more pressing.

She'd meant to renew when her financial situation improved. That hadn't happened yet.

Her shoulders slumped as she mentally reviewed her options. She couldn't afford a repair service, especially with the rest of her rent payment looming. A garage, however, would patch the tire for only a few dollars. If she could get the tire there.

The only solution was to switch out of her work clothes and change the flat herself. She dug into her purse, slipped an antacid tablet into her mouth and took a deep breath. She wasn't a helpless female. She knew about lugnuts and jacks and spare tires.

She could do this. She could. After all, how hard could it be to change a flat tire?

"You lousy lugnut. You think you're going to get the better of me, don't you? Think again, you blasted nut."

As Chase crossed the parking lot of the townhouse complex, he heard the low muttering before he saw the woman crouched on the pavement. The rear end of her car was jacked off the ground, and the woman wrestled with a lug wrench. A large rock was mysteriously wedged next to the tire.

His eyebrows raised. In his experience, women didn't change tires. Instead, they waited around for a man to do it for them. No matter that this woman was having trouble completing the task. She had his ultimate respect for attempting it.

Her back was to him, her hair color obscured by a baseball cap pulled low on her head. She was bent over so that her worn jeans hugged one of the most sweetly rounded bottoms he'd ever seen. He wondered if the front of her looked as good as the back. There was one sure way to find out.

"Need any help?"

Balancing on the balls of her feet, she turned around. Chase felt as though he'd been sucker punched. A lock of golden hair had escaped from the cap and dangled near her blue, determined eyes. Across her cheek was a swipe of black grease.

Michelle.

The woman who dressed like she belonged in a fashion magazine was the same one who'd taken on the flat tire by herself. He should have guessed it, but somehow he hadn't.

"Oh, no," she moaned, a greeting that did nothing for his ego. "Is it five o'clock already?"

"Nearly." He spread his hands, unable to resist making a point. "And here I am. In the flesh. Like I promised."

Something flashed in her eyes. "Don't bait me, Fletcher. I have better things to do than argue with you."

"I can see that." He nodded at the flat. "What I'm wondering is why Jason isn't helping you."

"Jason's not here." She brushed the hair back from her eyes and succeeded in getting another smear of grease on her face, this time across the nose. "He's working on a school project with a classmate. I was supposed to pick him up fifteen minutes ago, but I got sidetracked."

"I'd be happy to help." Chase crouched down beside her, exactly where he wanted to be. Even with grease on her face, her skin was pale and creamy at the same time. The delicate scent of peaches overrode the smell of tire rubber.

"Thanks for the offer, Boy Scout, but I can do this myself," she said, returning to the task. Four lugnuts were beside her on the ground, and she was working feverishly on the fifth, her arm muscles straining as she turned the wrench.

"You're in the way," she said after a moment.

"Sorry," he said, but he wasn't. He wanted to stay in her way until she looked at him the way she had in the planetarium. Calling himself a fool, he stood up and crossed his arms over his chest. In a few seconds, he'd solved the mystery of the rock. She'd wedged it against the tire in an effort to keep the tire from spinning.

"I bet you're wondering why that lugnut's so hard to get off."

"No more than I wondered about the other four," Michelle said, clenching her teeth as she worked the wrench, "and I got *them* off."

"You're supposed to loosen the lugnuts *before* you jack up the car. It's easier to get them off that way. Then you wouldn't need that rock."

"Now you tell me," she muttered, finally loosening the last bolt. She stood up, wiped her palms on her already dirty jeans and then positioned her hands on the tire. It took all his willpower not to volunteer to remove the tire for her.

She tugged, and he was glad he hadn't. The force of her effort propelled her backward, straight into his body. His hands automatically came out to steady her, cradling her hips as she regained her balance.

"Are you sure you don't want me . . ." He paused significantly as he bent down and whispered in her ear. ". . . to help."

He felt her full-body shiver before she wrenched away from him. "I'm sure. Why do men always assume that a woman needs their help?" Her words were tough, but her voice was shaky. Good. Chase didn't want to be the only one experiencing this crazy chemistry. She picked up the spare and positioned it over the wire wheel, shoving it in place. "We may be the weaker sex, but we're not helpless."

"It's called common courtesy," Chase said, even though he suspected it was much more than that. "I've changed a tire a dozen times. I bet this is your first."

"So what if it is?" she asked, going to work on the lugnuts.

"Don't tighten them all the way."

She looked at him, exasperated. "Can't you be quiet and let me do this my own way?"

"Only if you want to make things harder on yourself."

She didn't reply, but he noticed she took his advice. That was a small consolation. He shoved his hands in his pockets, feeling helpless. He did admire Michelle. She was self-sufficient and capable. What's more, she'd managed to raise a son to the ripe age of eleven without help from anyone, as far as he could see.

But, damn it, he wanted to help her. He wanted her to need him. Wanted it quite desperately. Standing here like this doing nothing but watching while she changed the flat went against his grain.

When she was finally finished, she tossed the jack in the trunk and rolled the flat tire to the back of the car.

"I don't suppose you'll let me lift that for you," he said nonchalantly, as though it didn't matter.

"You suppose right." Her back muscles strained as

she picked up the tire and lowered it into the trunk. It took her twice the time, and twice the effort, it would have taken him to complete the same task. Finally finished, she dusted off her hands.

"There," she said, turning and walking toward her townhouse. "Give me a minute to change, and then I'll run by and get Jason. You can wait in the living room until we get back."

He shook his head in disbelief and followed her. What would it take to get her to let him help her? "If you tell me where he is, I'll get him."

"No, I'll get him."

She opened the door to her townhouse and he followed her inside. He had the impression of a small, tidy place decorated in warm, homey colors but he was more interested in her aggravating behavior.

"So me picking Jason up goes against your no-helping-me-out rule, too?" he asked.

Michelle visibly bristled as she stopped walking and turned to face him. "I don't have a no-helping-me-out rule," she said.

"Then why did I just watch you change a flat?"

"It was my tire and my problem."

"You could have at least let me put the tire in the trunk. Whether you like it or not, I'm stronger than you. It would have been easier for me."

"Oh, I can accept that," she said, putting up a hand. "I also know that when someone offers help, it's because they want something in return."

His temper flared, the way only Michelle seemed to be able to ignite it. "Is it really so hard for you to accept that all I want is the satisfaction of helping you?"

"Yes," she snapped. "Don't forget. I was there when you kissed me the other night."

"You kissed me back," he pointed out.

Her chin came up. "You kissed me first."

"So let me get this right. You're saying I had some sort of payment in mind? Like a change-a-flat-tire-for-a-kiss scheme? Is that it?" Too late, he realized he'd raised his voice.

"I've seen the way you look at me," she retorted. "I wouldn't put it past you."

"Let me tell you something, honey," he said, advancing and capturing her chin in one hand. She glared at him, but didn't pull away. The set of her mouth was mutinous. "I don't need to blackmail you into kissing me. All I have to do is ask."

"Ha." Disbelief dripped from her laugh, but her expression didn't look quite so assured. Her uncertainty puffed up his ego, making him sure he was right. "You're unbelievably arrogant," she added. "And incredibly wrong."

"Oh, yeah?" he asked, gentling his fingers on her chin.

"Yeah," she replied tartly.

In answer, he put his hands on either side of her smooth cheeks and lowered his head. Slowly. Inch by inch. Centimeter by centimeter. Their eyes locked, and he watched hers turn a darker shade of blue, watched himself in her pupils. Her breathing was fast and shallow, like his own. Her breaths caressed his lips. It took an incredible effort to stop his forward motion, but he did. Her perfect pink mouth was barely an inch away.

"Kiss me," he said. It sounded like an order, but it felt like a plea. His gut was clenched in frustration, his muscles straining with the effort of keeping himself apart from her. Although it was a marvelous fall day, with a brisk bite in the air, his skin felt as though it were blistering.

"I said kiss me, Michelle." At the last instant, when he feared her contrary nature might give her the impetus to pull away, he added the word screaming in his heart, "please."

She shifted, a nearly imperceptible movement that brought her luscious mouth flush against his. At the contact, a deep, masculine sound, somewhere between a groan and a sigh, escaped him. She kissed him once, almost chastely, on the corner of his mouth, then moved to the middle, the other side, pressing sweet kisses as she went. He opened his mouth and drank in her breath, shuddering at the first tentative touch of her tongue on his lips. Almost shyly, her tongue ventured farther inside his mouth until it met his.

Something inside Chase broke, like a snapped rubber band. What began as a way to prove a point quickly turned into something much more elemental. Need. He didn't only want to kiss her back. He needed to.

He deepened the kiss, meeting her passion, reveling in the joyful little sound she made far back in her throat. He moved his hands to her nape, somehow dislodging her baseball cap. Glorious silken-blond hair spilled over his fingers, heightening his sensations.

She was heaven to kiss. A combination of boldness and passion tempered with a hint of shyness. The same sensations that had flowed through him inside the planetarium returned, making him long to complete what they'd started.

A car horn honked. Once, then twice. It was outside the townhouse but sounded as though it was no more than twenty yards away. He became aware of daylight streaming through her screen door, of birds singing, of a door slamming. Damn. They couldn't do this. Not now. Not here. He broke off the kiss, but kept his forehead pressed against hers.

"Two-twenty-five Chestnut Lane," she whispered after a moment, making about as much sense as making out in the middle of the day.

"Huh?"

"It's where Jason is." She sounded shaky, reminding him that he wasn't the only one having trouble gathering his wits. "Two-twenty-five Chestnut Lane."

His confusion cleared. She was telling him he could pick Jason up, allowing him, in one very small way, to help her. Elation swirled through him, but he tempered it with reality. She was right not to trust him too much. He wanted her—he couldn't deny that—but he couldn't promise her tomorrow. Not unless he was willing to make the same mistake twice.

"What time should I have him back?"

"I'll make it a point to be back here by six-thirty."

"Fine," he said. His hands were on her arms, making a gentle up-and-down motion. He should stop touching her, but he didn't want to. With their foreheads kissing, he felt connected to her.

"When you bring Jason home, I don't think you should come inside," she whispered. The soft words rushed through him like a chill in the air, demonstrating exactly why he should let her go.

He did so reluctantly, straightening to his full height and backing away inch by painful inch. In her eyes, he saw the same desire he knew was burning in his.

"I don't think I should come in, either," he agreed.

But, oh, how he wanted to.

Dani White whooped, threw up her arms and launched into a hip-rolling, shoulder-shaking dance. "Way to go, Benny Joe," she yelled.

Beside her in the stands, Michelle laughed and tugged on the PTA president's oversized T-shirt. "Dani," she whispered loudly, "that was a foul ball."

"I know." Dani sat back down on the hard-pine bleacher and grinned. "But I believe in positive feedback. My son hit, therefore I cheer."

Jason's and Benny Joe's team, the Yellowjackets, were up to bat. The baseball diamond, its dirt recently swept and white lines imperfectly drawn, shone in the afternoon sun. A refreshing fall breeze blew over the scene.

Michelle didn't know or care much about baseball, but she tried not to miss any of Jason's games. She'd rearranged her schedule today, cutting her open house an hour short, to be here for the opening pitch. For nearly two blissful hours, she'd done nothing except watch her son play and talk to Dani White. She hadn't even worried about what she could pawn to make the rent payment.

"You'll get 'em next time, slugger," Dani yelled as her son struck out. She obviously believed in the power of encouraging words just as much as positive feedback.

Michelle smiled. She'd been pleasantly surprised when Dani flagged her down and invited her to sit next to her. After what happened at the science museum, she hadn't expected that. But Dani had been friendly and talkative, tactfully refraining from mentioning Principal Goodman, and Michelle found herself liking her more and more.

Dani was the epitome of the suburban stay-at-home mom. Her backpack was filled with snacks, books and toys, everything she needed to keep her younger son, who played in the dirt nearby, occupied. She wore a Yellowjackets T-shirt she'd made herself by sewing on yellow-and-black appliqués. She confided to Michelle that she already had dinner cooking in the crockpot, vegetables and potatoes included.

She was everything Michelle wasn't. Everything, in fact, that Chase was searching for. The thought tugged at Michelle's spirits, trying to drag them down. Michelle couldn't have Chase, she knew that. But she didn't want anyone else to have him either, not even someone as nice as the widowed Dani White.

"Oooo la la," exclaimed the mother sitting on Dani's other side, whom Dani had introduced as Gay. "Who is that hunk of gorgeous man Jason's waving to?"

Michelle looked up and forgot to breathe when she saw that the hunk of gorgeous man was Chase. It was as though her thoughts had conjured him up out of thin air. He was walking from the parking lot toward the stands in that sexy take-your-time amble of his. The sun seemed to heat up twenty degrees. Or maybe it was Michelle's skin, flaming from the inside out. Ivan Pavlov had called it reflex behavior.

I see, therefore I want.

Chase's T-shirt wasn't particularly tight, but she could make out the muscular contours of his chest. His long legs were covered in denim, but she wanted them bare, exposed to her gaze. The same way as his even-featured, strong-jawed face and flyaway dark hair.

She was as bad as Pavlov's dogs. If someone rang a bell, she'd probably drool.

"That hunk of gorgeous man, my dear married friend, is Chase Fletcher," Dani White answered, her high-pitched voice sounding faintly breathless. "Single dad extraordinaire."

"Hey, I'm married, not dead," Gay said, fluffing out her bottle-red hair. "Just because you two are single doesn't mean you own the patent on ogling. I can look, even if I can't touch."

You better not touch, Michelle thought. Dani giggled, and Michelle realized she'd directed her silent warning at the wrong woman. Unlike Gay, Dani wasn't bound by any restrictions when it came to single men. By all accounts, she'd finished grieving for her late husband and wasn't averse to remarrying. What's more, Dani, not Gay, was the domestic goddess. Not to mention cute as the proverbial button.

"What I don't understand is what he's doing here," Dani continued. "I've never seen him at one of these games before. He only has the one daughter."

The daughter who was lagging behind her father, her arms crossed over her chest, her mouth unsmiling. Lauren obviously didn't want to be anywhere near a game that involved Jason. Or Jaaaaasooooon, as she'd called him.

"Show your stuff, Jason," she heard Chase yell, and realized her son was at the plate, a fact that had escaped her entirely. The pitcher went into a windup. Jason, his elbow raised and hips thrust forward, gave a mighty swing.

The ball pinged off his aluminum bat and sailed into the outfield on a rope of air, falling between the center- and left-fielders and dribbling to the fence. Michelle sprang to her feet as Jason rounded first base and went into second with a stand-up double.

Her gaze connected with Chase's. He was beaming, as proud as she was. As though it was their son, and not hers alone, who had gotten the hit. Before her imagination could run wild, she firmly reminded herself that Jason was not Chase's son. The boy's own father hadn't taken an interest in him. She wouldn't believe Chase's interest was anything more than passing.

"That's the longest ball Jason's hit all season," Dani remarked.

"Chase took him to the batting cage the other day to give him some tips on hitting," Michelle explained absently.

"Oh, so that's how it is." Gay's innuendo-filled voice made Michelle realize what she was doing. Grinning. Like an infatuated idiot. She tried to pull her eyes away from Chase but couldn't. He was headed straight for her.

"No. That's not how it is. I'm hardly his type," Michelle denied, then could have kicked herself. She was all but leaving the path clear for Dani. She thought about amending her statement, but Chase was already climbing the bleachers, and she forgot what she was going to say.

"Hey, Michelle," he said, fixing her with that bone-melting smile of his. Her idiotic grin reappeared. Chase's eyes lingered on her, before he turned to Dani and Gay.

"Ladies," he said. Dani introduced Gay, who nearly swooned when he shook her hand. Not that Chase seemed to notice. He dropped down next to Michelle, his broad shoulder brushing hers. Electricity crackled, sparks igniting in Michelle's every pore.

She was dimly aware of a batter striking out to end the inning and of Gay asking Dani about a recipe for a kid-friendly chicken casserole. But she was past paying close attention to anyone, or anything, but Chase.

He leaned toward her, his jaw so smoothly shaven she longed to stroke it, his breath smelling faintly of wintergreen. It reminded her of the last time they'd been together, reminded her of that sizzling kiss. He'd been so decent about it, never once pointing out she hadn't been able to resist the temptation of his lips. Making it clear it was just as impossible for him to resist hers.

Maybe she should employ that turnabout-is-fair-play cliché, and ask *him* to kiss *her*. Of course, if he asked her first, she wouldn't have to.

"That was a great hit. How's Jason done the rest of the game?" His question brought her back to earth with a crashing thud. He'd come to see Jason. Not her.

She shook off her daze, praying he hadn't noticed it. "He's playing catcher for the first time. Otherwise, he's walked twice and singled. This is the last inning, so that was probably his last at-bat."

"Lauren won't last more than an inning anyway." Chase nodded toward his daughter. Lauren was sitting alone on the bottom bleacher, looking sullen. "She's disgusted that we stopped by at all. She still refers to Jason as 'that beastly boy'."

"He calls her 'that ghastly girl'."

"That's not bad," Chase said, laughing. "They might even top us when it comes to making up insulting names for each other."

"Don't you dare start that La Belle Michelle stuff, Maddening Man," Michelle warned, waving her finger. His eyes crinkled in amusement as they shared their private joke.

Reluctantly, because she couldn't keep staring at Chase, Michelle turned her attention back to the field. Jason was behind the plate, sneaking a glimpse at Lauren. He readied to catch the next pitch a second late and reacted too slowly when the pitcher sent the ball into the dirt. He got a glove out in front of him, but the ball glanced off it, hitting him directly in the groin before ricocheting to the ground.

"That's gotta hurt," Gay intoned at the same time that Michelle covered her face with her hands. She couldn't look. Not with her son in pain. A smattering of applause brought her out of her trance.

Jason was up and walking gingerly, but he seemed to be all right. Which didn't make sense. Hadn't the ball just hit the most sensitive part of his anatomy?

"Relax. He's protected," Chase said, touching her arm. "He told me he was playing catcher today. So after we went to the batting cage, I bought him an athletic cup."

"You what?" Her eyebrows shot up. Chase should have brought Jason straight home. She'd made it clear she didn't want them indulging in any more male bonding. She felt the first tell-tale signs of a nose quiver.

"Stop it with the nose already," Chase whispered for her ears alone. "He asked me, Michelle. What was I supposed to do? Refuse?"

Yes, Michelle almost shouted. Except she knew that was unrealistic. She wanted to guard against Jason becoming too attached to Chase, but she didn't want her son to develop a complex in the process.

"He should have asked me to buy him one instead," Michelle said, trying to calm herself down.

"It's not exactly the same thing as asking you to buy him an ice cream. He's eleven years old, you're his mom and he was embarrassed." He reached over, touched her cheek, looked deeply into her eyes. "It doesn't matter who bought it for him. As long as he has one. Okay?"

She took a shaky breath, because Chase didn't understand. It did matter. Despite all her best efforts, it drove home the point that there were some things she couldn't do for her son. Things a man could do better.

Such as buying him an athletic cup and teaching him how to hit a baseball.

"Let it go, Michelle. I'm not going to let you pick a fight with me about this one."

For the rest of the inning, Michelle sat next to Chase in silence while he explained some of the finer points of baseball to Dani and Gay. Both women were annoyingly appreciative, giving him their full attention and laughing whenever he said anything even the slightest bit amusing.

Chase was a charmer, that was for sure. As much at ease with adoring females as with an impressionable eleven-year-old boy who thought he hung the moon because he'd played baseball. She frowned. The baseball association wasn't all there was to this connection Jason was developing with Chase. He was a boy who'd never had a father, and Chase was treating him like a son.

"Oh, Chase, you are too much." Dani giggled, bringing Michelle's attention back to their conversation. Except she didn't know what they were talking about. "Where have you been all my life?"

"Probably sitting in the back of the room at the PTA meeting, admiring the president," he quipped.

He and Dani shared a smile, which brought home the fact to Michelle that Dani just might be his dream woman. She was the epitome of a domestic goddess, which was what he was looking for. No wonder he was flirting with her.

"Not as much as the women there were admiring you, I'd bet," Dani said. Gay nodded vigorously, adding credence to Dani's comment.

Dani, Gay and Chase stood up, making Michelle wonder why. Then she noticed members of the two teams running toward each other for the post-game handshake. The game was over. She assumed Jason's team had won. At least they'd been winning before her mind had gone haywire.

"Great finish, huh?" Chase said, putting a hand on her back to guide her down the bleachers after Dani and Gay started talking to some other parents. It was an oddly proprietorial gesture, one she liked a little too much. In self-defense, she moved out of his reach. "Jason'll be thrilled about scoring the winning run," he added.

So the Yellowjackets had won, something she could read on her son's face when he came jogging toward them.

"Hey, Chase," Jason called, ignoring the fact that she was standing next to him. "You were right. I was dropping my elbow when I swung. I owe that hit to you."

"Oh, no, you don't, sport. You did it all yourself," Chase said. One of his teammates called to Jason that the coach was having a post-game meeting, and Chase nodded toward the celebrating group. "Catch you later, Jase. Go enjoy your victory."

Chase? Jase? This was worse than she thought. They'd already dispensed with formality. Chase grinned and gave the boy a double thumbs-up. Jason grinned back before running off to join his team. That did it. She needed to put a stop to this right now. She took a deep breath.

"I want to make sure we've got this straight about

Jason," she said. Chase cocked his head, looking so handsome she almost hit him. "This thing you've started with him has to stop right here. No more buying him things. No more trips to the batting cage."

Chase stroked his chin, regarding her as though she were a particularly puzzling mathematical equation. "That's gonna be a problem," he said slowly, "since I promised to take him again tomorrow."

"You what?" she sputtered, then lowered her voice to his level. In and out. In and out. She had to remember to breathe. She felt a sneeze coming on. She could take care of herself, but Jason was so open, so trusting, so in need of her protection. "I told you I didn't want you making any more promises to my son."

Chase was unprepared for the way his chest constricted, as though an invisible vise had it in its grip. By rejecting his help, she was rejecting him. It shouldn't hurt, but it did. He forced himself to shrug. "All I'm doing is helping him with his hitting."

"But I don't want you to," she said, so loudly that some of the people walking away from the bleachers turned and looked back at them. Then she sneezed.

Out of the corner of his eye, Chase spotted Lauren regarding them with interest. He ran a hand over his mouth and stifled the urge to yell back at Michelle. Logically, he realized he wanted to lash out because she'd hurt him. But she was looking at him with huge, haunted eyes, as though she was the one who'd been hurt.

He watched the uneven rise and fall of her chest, wondering what was going on here. This was the same inexplicably extreme reaction she'd had the other day at his house. Obviously, it involved a hell of a lot more than the simple promise he'd made to Jason. He pulled a handkerchief out of his pocket and handed it to her, but she didn't take it.

"You still haven't explained why taking your son to the batting cage is such a big deal," he said, silently congratulating himself for keeping his voice level.

"We're doing fine just the way we are, Jason and me," she continued, breathing hard. "We don't need another man in our lives making promises he never intends to keep."

That was it, Chase thought. He was paying for the sins of another man. Maybe even other men. The remnants of his anger died in his chest.

"Is that what this is all about, Michelle?" he asked, gentling his voice. "Are you talking about your ex-husband? Or was there someone else who did this number on you?"

Her face went white and her jaw quivered an instant before she got control of herself and put her armor back in place.

"That," she said, poking him once in the chest with her index finger, "is none of your business."

He sighed. He wanted to know what had happened, but now wasn't the time to press. "The promise I made to your son," he pointed out, "is my business."

"Not anymore, it's not." She moved away from him, her nose still quivering. "I'll explain to Jason that you can't make it tomorrow."

"You can't do that," he protested, the anger he thought extinguished flaring in his chest like an inferno. "Then he'll think I broke my promise."

"Better now than later," she tossed over her shoulder and walked away from him.

If Lauren hadn't been there, watching them with far too much interest, he would have followed her. That he couldn't was undoubtedly a good thing, because the only way to keep from throttling Michelle was to keep away from her.

Far, far away. From here on out, he wouldn't go anywhere near her.

Chapter Seven

Michelle was so near that Chase could smell the subtle flowery scent of her perfume and hear her slightly uneven breaths. So near that, if he reached out, he could touch the smooth softness of her skin.

So near that it was driving him stark, raving mad.

He'd kept his promise to stay away from her for four days, but on the fifth Thurman Goodman had taken the matter out of his control.

In a bad case of déjà vu, the Starlight Pond principal sat behind his impressive oak desk with scowling lips and narrowed eyes. The only differences were his bow tie was dotted instead of striped and he seemed a little scared. He probably feared they'd throw something at each other besides insults.

He eyed the globe of the world on Mr. Goodman's desk. If he were a different type of man, he just might make the principal's fear come true. After the way

Michelle had made sure he broke his promise to Jason, he was certainly justified.

"I must say I'm quite vexed to see you two in my office again," the principal said, pushing up the nose of his glasses. They were still held together with masking tape. Obviously, the replacement pair hadn't yet arrived. "I hoped you two would figure out a way for everyone to get along."

Michelle sent a dark look at Chase, as though it was his fault they kept arguing. She was dressed in another of her power suits, this one navy blue, but the dark circles that shaded her eyes looked less than professional. Good. He hoped she'd laid awake nights thinking of him the same way he'd laid awake thinking of her. When he wasn't thinking of disagreeing with her, he'd been thinking of kissing her. He swiped a hand across his forehead, trying to wipe away the thought. He focused on Mr. Goodman.

"You didn't call us in here to lecture us on getting along," Chase said. "Suppose you tell us why we *are* here."

"You're here because your children don't get along any better than the two of you," Thurman Goodman snapped, then folded his hands on the desk. He looked from Michelle to Chase as though he expected one of them to erupt. When neither did, he continued. "Would you like to hear what they did this time?"

"Not particularly," Michelle murmured, earning a grunt of dismay from the principal. She wet her delectable lips. "But I guess you're going to tell us anyway."

Mr. Goodman fixed his gaze on Michelle. "Your son, Ms. Germaine, scooped his chocolate pudding out of its cup and smeared it all over Lauren's face." The principal executed a sharp pivot so his chair faced Chase. "And your daughter, Mr. Fletcher, poured a carton of milk on top of Jason's head. She threw in a straw for good measure."

Chase started to speak at the same time as Michelle, but Mr. Goodman wasn't having any of it.

"Silence," he ordered, rapping the desk. "I will not listen to you two argue about who may have provoked whom. I do not know who started this food-fight travesty. And I do not care. I care about keeping order at Starlight Pond. Today is Wednesday. I am hereby suspending your children for the rest of today and all of Thursday and Friday."

"Three days?" Michelle exclaimed, putting trembling fingers to her lips. "Isn't that rather harsh?"

"Expulsion is harsh, Ms. Germaine. And that is what your children will face if they can not learn to get along."

"We've already tried talking to them," Chase said, looking to Michelle for confirmation. She nodded. In the space of a heartbeat, they'd gone from adversaries to allies. "What do you suggest we do next?"

"I've been puzzling over this, and I suggest the drastic approach." Mr. Goodman pursed his lips. "Your children should be made to spend time together. And not just sitting-in-front-of-the-television time. They need a cooperative activity where they can learn to work together toward a common good."

"Such as?" Chase asked.

"An ideal activity would be the fall cleanup campaign the Clean Fairfax Council is running," the principal answered. "All you have to do is pick a day, select a site and let the council know of your plans. They provide supplies."

"Sounds good to me." At this point, anything that would keep Lauren from getting an academic black mark sounded good to Chase. He turned to Michelle. "How about we do it tomorrow or Friday?"

"I can't," Michelle said, biting her lip. "I have to work."

So they were back to that again. Disappointment cut into Chase, so keen he couldn't stop from making a sarcastic response.

"I work, too," Chase pointed out, "but I'm not so wedded to my job that I can't take a day off for the good of my child."

Michelle's nose twitched, and her eyes flashed, telling him he'd hit the mark. "You get paid whether you work or not. I don't. I have five realtor open houses in the next two days to look over property. If I miss them, it could cost me sales."

What she said made sense, but, perversely, Chase didn't want to admit it. "So you're saying you can't do it?" he asked.

"I didn't say I couldn't do it," she responded tartly. "I said I couldn't do it Thursday or Friday."

"Or Saturday or Sunday either, right?" he asked.

"Listen, buster—"

"Oh, no. Oh, no. Don't start this again," Mr. Goodman interrupted. His upper body was bent, as though getting ready to duck under the desk to get out of any war path they happened to take. "Remember what I said. If your children are going to get along, you must, too."

"She's the one who won't commit to a date," Chase said.

"That's not true. I was about to—"

"How about Saturday?" Mr. Goodman interrupted. "You could see how it goes on that one day and leave Sunday open in case you need more time together."

"Fine with me," Chase said quickly. He slanted a challenging look at Michelle. "Would that work for you, Belle?"

Her nose quivered, but she did an admirable job of not sneezing. "My name's Michelle," she said finally. "And, yes, it'll work."

"Will wonders never cease! You agree," Mr. Goodman chimed in. "I must say I'm glad I won't be along. I've been in the line of fire before." He adjusted the broken glasses on his nose. "And it wasn't a pleasant experience."

Fat gray clouds spit cool drizzle over the parkland, dampening Michelle's already drooping spirits. They'd been clearing the park of litter most of the morning and part of the afternoon, and she'd been ready to pack up the litter bags and go home even before the rain hit.

The rain jackets they'd all put on didn't help matters. Her back still hurt from bending over, and her stomach still churned from worrying whether the client she'd put off would find another real-estate agent. Worst of all, her heart hurt from the prospect of explaining to Jason why she'd had to pawn their television.

"That's a sweet gum," she heard Chase say in that annoyingly cheerful tone he'd used for most of the day. He'd called the two children over to his side and was indicating a brilliantly colored, full-bodied tree. "Isn't she a beaut? She does best in full sun."

The look on his oh-too-handsome face was almost rapturous. He was wearing those faded jeans that showed off his long legs and tight behind, and he seemed oblivious to the drizzle. His thick mahogany hair was slightly wet, throwing his features into prominence. She hadn't noticed before just how high his cheekbones were. The mouth, wide and kissably delicious, she'd noticed.

"See those bushes over there with the purplish red leaves?" He pointed to some showy shrubs that nicely bracketed a park bench. "Those are Improved Double File Viburnums. In the spring, they have white flowers."

Jason hung on Chase's every word, as though he were giving a play-by-play commentary of an enthralling baseball game. Lauren seemed nonplused, her hands jammed in her pockets like she'd heard it all before. Michelle sent Chase a dark look and bent over to pick up a discarded hamburger wrapper.

Didn't he realize she was working here? That every time he stopped and waxed poetic on the wonders of the physical world was one more minute he could have spent picking up litter? Which was why they were there in the first place. Not that he seemed to know that. When he wasn't talking, he was as likely to be straightening decorative stones or picking weeds out of flower beds as he was cleaning up.

"The Japanese Snowball Viburnum also has the purplish-red leaves in the fall and white flowers in the spring," Chase continued. "But I prefer the Improved Double File, because—"

"Jason? Lauren?" Michelle called. It was either interrupt or scream. "There's a spot down by the lake that needs to be picked up. Why don't you take one of the litter bags and head over there?"

"How much longer do we have to do this?" Lauren asked, sending Jason one of the killing looks she'd been directing at him all day, as though it was his fault she was wasting her day picking up litter. Jason glared back at Lauren and muttered something under his breath Michelle was pretty sure was uncomplimentary. But she couldn't call him on it, because she hadn't heard what he said.

"We're almost finished," Chase said. His teeth flashed. The lout was actually smiling. "Just hang in there a little longer. You two do the area by the lake. Michelle and I'll finish up here."

Lauren rolled her eyes but didn't protest. Jason picked up one of the thirty-gallon bags the county had provided. They headed off together, separated by twenty feet of grass. Because of their history, Michelle had been careful to keep them in sight. As they disappeared over the crest of a hill, she had a moment's misgiving.

"She looks like she's been set on fire, doesn't she?" Chase intoned, diverting her attention. He was staring up at a stately tree with leaves of orange and gold.

"That's a Red Maple, which is superior to its cousin, the Silver Maple, because—"

"Would you stop it with the horticulture lesson already?" Michelle yelled. A damp strand of hair fell into her eyes, and she swiped it back. "We have litter to pick up here. What does it matter if that's an Orange Maple or a Gold Maple?"

"It's Red Maple and Silver Maple," he corrected. "And it matters because the Red Maple is an excellent specimen for parks because of its beauty and hardiness. The Silver Maple is more of a trash tree. Sure, it grows fast. But it sheds and it'll blow over in a storm."

She threw up her hands and tried not to sneeze. "You're doing this on purpose, aren't you?"

"Doing what?" he asked calmly. Why wasn't he yelling? She could deal with this much better if he were yelling.

"Making me crazy. That's what." She looked up at the sky. Raindrops hit her in the face, adding insult to irritation. "Don't you realize it's raining?"

"What does that have to do with anything?"

"We're picking up litter in the rain, and you're identifying bushes and trees and having a grand old time." She kicked out with one soggy tennis shoe, overturning a litter bag. "This isn't supposed to be fun."

Chase rubbed the back of his neck, the first sign that his composure was breaking. "Right about now, you're making sure that it's not."

"Good," she said. "I don't want you to have any fun."

Color danced in front of Chase's eyes more vivid

than the blazing fall foliage all around them. Michelle glared up at him with her beautiful, heart-shaped face, her luscious lower lip thrust petulantly forward.

He had a sudden, sharp urge to draw that lip into his mouth. He took a step forward, reached for her . . . and dropped his hands to his side. He couldn't be sure if he'd suckle her lip or bite it. Yelling back at her was easier and far less complicated. "Maybe I don't want you to have any fun, either."

She opened her delectable mouth, no doubt to blast him with another verbal assault, but it was Lauren's voice he heard. It rang out in the cool fall air, unmistakable in its hostility.

"Shut up or I'll stick you!"

Michelle's mouth closed. Her sea-blue eyes met his, alarmed instead of hostile. He pictured the sharply pointed litter pickup stick Lauren had been carrying and knew Michelle was imagining the same thing.

"You're nuts." Now it was Jason's voice that Chase heard. He was definitely not shutting up. "Completely bonkers. Grade-A whacko."

"Don't you see what I have in my hands?" Lauren was shouting again. "You should be afraid. You should be very afraid."

"Not again," Michelle muttered and took off in the direction the children had headed. In her high heels at the museum, she hadn't been able to keep with him. But in tennis shoes, she had sprinter's speed. He stumbled over a tree root, righting himself before he went sprawling, and they reached the children in a dead heat.

This time it was Chase and not Michelle who was

struck dumb. The children were standing at the edge of the man-made lake. Jason's back was to the water, and Lauren was advancing, threatening him with the pointed tip of her litter pickup stick.

"Lauren Fletcher, you put that stick down this instant," Michelle commanded before Chase could say anything. His daughter dropped the stick and turned startled eyes to Michelle. She obviously hadn't heard them coming. "What were you thinking? Pointing it at Jason like that?"

"Aw, I wasn't gonna poke him," Lauren said, scuffing her feet in the mud. "I just wanted to make him walk into the lake."

"You were too gonna poke me," Jason said.

"Was not!"

"Was too!"

"Stop it. This thing between the two of you has gone far enough. It's not acceptable behavior," Michelle said firmly. Chase looked at her with admiration. Where was the woman who'd confessed she felt inadequately prepared to cope with pre-teens? He couldn't have said it better himself.

"You should talk, Mom," Jason said, rolling his eyes in a gesture that brought to mind his mother. "You and Chase are even worse than we are."

"We are not," Chase protested.

"Are too," Lauren chimed in. "Did you think we didn't hear when you were yelling at each other about horticulture?"

"Yeah." Jason moved slightly closer to Lauren. He crossed his arms over his chest. Lauren did the same.

"Kids have ears. Don't forget we heard you outside the principal's office, too."

"And I know you broke Mr. Goodman's glasses," Lauren told Michelle.

Chase exchanged a helpless look with Michelle. Their children were right. They had said and done those things. Of course, they hadn't meant for Lauren and Jason to witness them. He sidled closer to Michelle, presenting a unified front.

"What your father and I do, Lauren, isn't any of your concern," Michelle said. "Or yours, Jason."

"It is when your arguments start messing up my life," Jason said. He'd edged even closer to Lauren. "Do you think I didn't figure out why Chase didn't take me to the batting cage Sunday? It was because you told him not to. That stinks, Mom. Just because you don't like him doesn't mean I can't."

"How could you not like my dad?" Lauren leaped to his defense, reminding Chase that loyalty was one of the benefits of having children. "Everybody likes my dad."

Jason jerked a finger at Chase. "Your dad doesn't like my mom, either. I betcha he wouldn't let you hang out with her."

Lauren whirled on Chase, her mouth tight. Loyalty, he thought, could only take you so far. "Is that why you told me I couldn't call and ask Ms. Germaine if she'd go shopping with me?"

Now it was Michelle's turn to whirl on Chase. "You told her she couldn't call me?"

"That's not quite the way it happened." Chase wondered why Michelle seemed upset. All he'd done was speak the truth. "I told her a busy woman like you wouldn't have time to take her shopping."

"But that's not true!"

"Sure, it is. You barely made time for today."

"But I did make time!"

"Only because you didn't have a choice."

"That's not true, either. I wanted to come today." Her nose gave a quiver, telling him he'd made her angry. Again. "What gives you the right to judge me? You're insufferable."

"Oh, I'm insufferable, am I?" The unfairness of her attack punctured him like a bee's stinger. "Well, you're intolerable."

He heard a snort of disgust, but it couldn't have come from Michelle, because she was in the midst of a string of sneezes.

"Let's get out of here, Jason," Lauren said, shaking her dark hair. "I don't want to listen to this."

"Me, neither." Jason picked up one side of the nearly full bag of litter and Lauren took the other. They stomped away, dragging it between them. Chase pulled his handkerchief out of his jeans pocket and handed it to Michelle. This time, she took it. He nodded toward their retreating children.

"That's the most cooperation they've shown all day," he commented. "Maybe there's hope for them yet."

He sat down on the thick trunk of a fallen tree and patted the space next to him. After a moment's hesitation, she joined him. The rain was falling a little harder now, splashing down on the lake with thousands of tiny, sparkling drops. The musty scent of leaves and wet earth filled the air.

"They're right, you know," Chase said. "We haven't been setting a very good example."

"Tell me about it," she said, wiping her nose. "I've sneezed more since I've met you than an allergy sufferer in a Kansas hayfield."

He chuckled. His anger was gone, washed away with the rain and the pleasure he got from her company. "Why do you think I started carrying a handkerchief?"

Her eyebrows rose. "For me?"

"For you," he answered, tapping her nose.

She sighed, and her eyes softened, like melting ice. "What I don't get is how you can be so aggravating one minute and so sweet the next."

"I know I'm sweet." He grinned. "But I hadn't realized I was aggravating. I thought that's what you were."

"Very funny." She rested a hand on one of her hips, and her elbow shot out at an angle. "*I* wasn't the one who kept up a running commentary all day on the flora and fauna of the park."

Had he done that? Chase thought back over the last few hours and had to concede she had a point. "I might have gotten a little carried away, but I haven't been here for a while. I guess I was kind of excited to see something I designed come to life."

"You designed this park?" Her voice rose an entire octave.

Chase nodded, looking around them and taking in the foot path that ran along the perimeter of the lake.

Before the rain, he'd gotten immense satisfaction from seeing how very many people used the path. "A lot of the landscape was already in place, of course, but this was my baby. I did the drawings and decided what kind of border plants would best suit what was already here. Then I came out here and supervised the project."

"But it's lovely."

"You sound surprised."

"No, it's not that . . . It's . . ." She stopped, covered her mouth with her hand and shook her head. "Why didn't you tell me you designed this park? You must think I'm an idiot, yelling at you like that when you have every right to be proud of what you did."

He touched her smooth cheek. She was wearing jeans, a red rain jacket and sneakers, with her hair shoved under a denim cap. She shouldn't have looked sexy, but she did. Then again, she always looked sexy. It didn't matter if her clothes were drenched and dotted with mud, if grease streaked her face, if her hair was hidden under a cap. He had only to look at her to want her.

He wanted her now, so much that he was starting to forget why he couldn't have her. Either that, or he didn't want to remember. "I've never thought you were an idiot, Michelle. A little huffy, maybe. But never idiotic."

"I used to think you were an idiot," she said, and he laughed.

"*Used to* better be the key words in that sentence."

"Oh, they are." Her sea-blue eyes were sincere. "Now that I know you better, I think you're okay."

"Only okay?"

"Well, let me put it this way," Michelle said and then spoke exactly what was on her mind. "I can't think of anybody I'd rather be sitting next to on a log in the rain after hours of picking up litter."

Michelle quickly averted her face so he couldn't see the stunned surprise she knew was written on her features. Because she'd spoken the truth. In the last few weeks, Chase Fletcher had somehow wiggled his way into her life and become important to her. Except she didn't want him to know that.

"So what are we going to do about our kids?" she asked, trying to change the subject.

"Our kids? We weren't talking about our kids."

"We are now," she said firmly.

"I'd rather talk about why I'm your choice for log sitting."

The corner of her mouth twitched, and a bubble of amusement rose in her throat. "I was right. You are insufferable."

"But nice to sit next to on a log."

She felt her face flame, and he grinned. It made tiny, well-used lines appear around his mouth and eyes, brightening them, brightening the rainy day. He slung an arm around her and squeezed her shoulder, drawing her closer. It was the most natural thing in the world to let his arm stay exactly where it was.

He gave a theatrical sigh. "Okay, okay. We'll talk about that some other time. But right now, you're right. We need to talk about our kids."

"Assuming, of course, that they're not off somewhere killing each other," Michelle said. "Thus eliminating the need."

He chuckled, and she felt the sound reverberate through her body. "They looked almost chummy just now," he said. "They also have a point. We can't expect them to get along if we don't."

"So what do we do?"

His fingertips danced on her shoulder, sending little shivers the length of her body. "We get along," he answered, his warm breath close to her ear.

"Hah." Even to Michelle, her exclamation sounded breathless. No doubt because their bodies were pressed together from shoulder to thigh, and her heart was thump-thump-thumping. "How are we going to manage that? We can't possibly get along."

"Sure, we can."

"Can not," she whispered.

He nuzzled the soft skin of her neck, his mouth warm, wet and wonderful. "Can, too," he whispered back.

Oh, boy. A languid warmth spread through Michelle, weighing down her chest, making her limbs limp. They'd been talking about something important, but at the moment she couldn't remember what. His mouth trailed from her neck up to her ear, and she knew she'd be beyond thought if she didn't move away from him. *Move*, she told herself. *Move*.

Fingers ran softly, sensuously over her lips, coming to rest at the side of her face. She was still facing the lake, although she was beyond seeing it. Ever so gently, those fingers turned her head toward the mouth that was doing such fabulous things to her sensitive skin.

Move, she told herself again. *Move before it's too late.*

This time, her body obeyed. She anchored a hand on the log and got to her feet, escaping his arms, evading his lips, denying herself what she wanted far, far too much. Her legs were so wobbly she had trouble standing.

He sat back, watching her through hooded eyes. He was thoroughly wet now, his hair sleek and dark. The rain seemed to have wiped his features clean of pretense. He wanted her. She could see it in the set of his mouth, in the smoke of his eyes. She also understood that this time, he was going to let her go. He wasn't making any promises about next time.

"What were you saying," he asked softly, "about us not being able to get along?"

She swallowed and tried to think. Now that he wasn't touching her, she should be able to manage that. The problem was that he was still looking at her, imprinting her body with his eyes. She pulled up the hood of her rain slicker, trying to hide from him, but it offered scant coverage. His eyes didn't leave her. She couldn't speak.

"What we need to do is show Lauren and Jason we can get along," Chase said after a minute. Michelle's mouth dropped open. Was he actually proposing what she thought he was proposing?

"But we can't let them see us kissing," she protested. He laughed then, a great belly laugh that drowned out the sound of the raindrops hitting the lake.

"Oh, Belle, that was priceless. I meant we should show them we can compromise."

"Of course you did," Michelle said, trying to recover. That's why, she told herself, she didn't scold him for calling her Belle. Not because she liked the sound of it on his lips.

"You lift your ban on me taking Jason to the batting cage, and I'll let you take Lauren shopping."

Something warm and feminine inside Michelle leaped at the prospect of taking Lauren shopping, but she still worried about the attachment Jason was forming to Chase. It couldn't be good for him, could it?

"What do you say?" Chase asked. "Come on, Michelle. You can trust me."

"You won't make him any promises you can't keep?"

"I won't," he said solemnly. "And I assume you'll do the same for Lauren."

"I wouldn't lie to Lauren," Michelle said, then bit her lip. "I only hope I don't disappoint her. I've never taken a young girl shopping before."

"Disappoint her?" He gave a short laugh. "How can you disappoint her? You have terrific taste."

"You think I have terrific taste?"

"Look at you," he said, sweeping a hand to encompass her blue jeans and ruby rain jacket. "Even when you're soaking wet, you're beautiful."

Her breath hitched. For a moment, she could barely breathe. Male appreciation shone in his eyes. "You think I'm beautiful?" she parroted. Stupidly.

"Yes, you have terrific taste," he said, getting up from the log. "Yes, you're beautiful. Yes, I'll owe you big if you take over the dreaded task of taking Lauren shopping."

They stood there for a moment looking at each other. It was all Michelle could do not to walk into arms she knew would open for her. "So what now?" she asked.

He offered a smile and a hand. They both took a step forward, meeting each other halfway. Their hands linked in a warm grasp.

"We find the kids, and take them out for burgers." He paused significantly, wagging his eyebrows at her. "And we try as hard as we can not to kiss in front of them."

Chapter Eight

The giggles drifting from the open window of Michelle's townhouse were even louder than the catchy Latin beat of the music. Chase paused in his approach, shamelessly eavesdropping.

"No, not like that." It was Lauren's voice, high-pitched and happy. "Your motion's too jerky. You need to swing your hips like this, more circular."

"Like this?" He could barely make out Michelle's voice through her laughter.

"Good, good! Yeah, that's it." Lauren shouted to be heard over the music, and then both females sang along to the chorus of the song, startlingly off-key.

Chase smiled. Then he laughed. If Michelle knew he was outside the window listening, she'd probably be appalled. But this was a side of her he hadn't seen before, and he wasn't about to feel guilty. If there hadn't been a beautiful flowering camellia bush in

135

front of the window, he would have peeked inside and added the offense of Peeping Tom to eavesdropper.

He waited until the song ended to ring the doorbell, then had to ring it again before the volume dipped on the stereo and the door yanked open.

"Hi, Dad." Lauren, pink-cheeked and breathless, stood in the foyer. The hair she usually kept in a ponytail was loose around her shoulders in a stylish cut that feathered around her face. She was wearing bell-bottom jeans and a cropped sweater that she'd bought on her shopping spree with Michelle. She did a pirouette, her hair swinging along with her. "What do you think?"

"I think," he said, taking her by the shoulders and planting a sound kiss on her forehead, "that you look beautiful."

Lauren brought her hands to her face. Her usually unadorned fingernails were painted a glittery pink. "Isn't it the best haircut? I told Michelle I wanted my hair to look like hers, so she took me to her beauty shop. It's not exactly the same, with me being so much younger and all. But it's way cool, don't you think? Isn't she the absolute best?"

He lifted his gaze from his daughter's flushed, pretty face to the woman trailing her to the door. He had to press his lips together so he wouldn't salivate. A sleek pair of black leggings outlined Michelle's proportionally long limbs and perfectly rounded hips. She'd tied her T-shirt at the waist, and her hair, usually so neat, was in wild disarray. She was flushed and breathless, the same way she was after they kissed. Their eyes locked.

"She's the absolute best thing I've seen in a very long time," he said deliberately, honestly. Michelle licked her bottom lip the way he wanted to, flushed an even deeper shade of red and untied her T-shirt with fumbling fingers. It dropped to mid-thigh, covering most of her luscious curves.

Lauren took his hand and drew him into the townhouse, shutting the door behind them. The music with the infectious Latin beat was still playing, much softer than before.

"Wait until you see what Michelle gave me," Lauren chattered on, oblivious to the undercurrents flowing between the two adults. She plucked a set of earrings from the side table in the room where she and Michelle had been dancing and held them up. Miniature dolphins dangled from them. "Aren't they cool? Of course, I can't wear them unless you let me get my ears pierced. Can I, Dad? Michelle said she'd take me to the mall next week to have it done if it's okay with you."

"I don't see why not," Chase said and was unprepared when Lauren flung herself into his arms. She stood on tiptoe and pulled his head down so she could kiss him on the cheek.

"Thank you, thank you, thank you," she gushed, then drew back when a horn sounded outside the townhouse. "That must be Darcy's mother coming to pick me up for the movie."

Chase cocked his head, because that did not compute. "Wait a minute. Wasn't I supposed to pick you up and drive you to Darcy's? You said you were leaving for the movie from there."

"Change of plans. I called to tell you, but Grandpa said you'd already left. Sorry." Lauren kissed him again and then skipped across the room and gave Michelle a warm hug. Chase's heart stopped. They looked so perfect together. The pretty blond pixie and his high-spirited brunette daughter, who was already as tall as Michelle.

"Thanks bunches and bunches, Michelle," Lauren said, planting a kiss on Michelle's cheek. "I'll call you tomorrow and tell you what the kids at school said about my new haircut."

Michelle smiled and ruffled her hair. "On you, how could they not love it?"

The horn sounded again, and Lauren rushed around the room, gathering her belongings. "Bye, Michelle. Bye, Dad," she called, and a moment later she was gone and they were alone.

"Whew," Chase said, theatrically wiping his brow. "I'm tired after just talking to her."

Michelle smiled and walked over to the stereo to turn the music off. He wondered what she'd say if he asked her to tie up her shirt again so he could get another look at all those luscious curves. A man, he felt sure, hadn't invented thigh-long T-shirts.

"Lauren has a lot of energy," Michelle said. "When she's not directing it at Jason, she's a delight."

"I think they've been doing better, don't you? I didn't get any calls this week from Mr. Goodman."

"Neither did I," Michelle said, "and I thought I heard Jason grunt when Lauren nodded at him today. Actual words, like hello and goodbye, might come next."

"Considering some of the things they say to each other, it might be better if they don't talk."

"We're talking," Michelle pointed out, then pressed her lips together when she read the truth in his chocolate-brown eyes. She knew as well as he did that they couldn't stop talking. If they did, they'd wind up in each other's arms.

"Yeah," he said gruffly. "I dropped Jason at Benny Joe's on the way over here. Dani asked me to tell you not to pick him up until after dinner. She's making Benny Joe's favorite, and she wants Jason to try it."

"What's Benny Joe's favorite?"

"Steak Deion, I think she called it." He screwed up his forehead. "No, wait a minute. Deion's a pro athlete. It was Steak something else."

"Steak Diane," Michelle supplied while her spirits plummeted. No way could she cook anything that sounded as sophisticated as that. Not even if she took a course in gourmet cooking, which she didn't have time for anyway.

What else had her domestic-goddess friend and Chase talked about? She wondered if Dani had invited him over later in the week for some gourmet dining for two, then reminded herself it couldn't matter. She and Chase were friends, which is as far as she could let their relationship progress.

They'd both been crystal clear about their needs. He wanted to marry a woman who'd make family her career while she wanted a career that would let her single-handedly provide for her family. The problem was that her traitorous body also wanted him.

He was blocking the entry to the hall, looking tall

and appealing and impossibly sexy. The blood running through her veins seemed to hike a notch in temperature, and liquid heat pooled low in her stomach. She cleared her throat. She shouldn't be alone with him like this in her townhouse, with no one to chaperone. No how. No way.

"So I guess you need to go," she blurted out.

He shrugged his impossibly broad shoulders and she wondered what they'd look like if she stripped off his shirt. Marvelous, she suspected. Like sculpted perfection. She'd gotten that impression in the planetarium when he'd kissed her and she'd clung to them. "Not really," he said.

Not really? Oh, boy. This was bad. Really bad. How was she supposed to maintain this friendship if they were cooped up in her townhouse together? Didn't he know that the only way they could truly be friends was if they kept a certain distance between them? A distance greater than the twelve inches that now separated them. She stepped back.

"I think you do need to go."

He stepped forward. He smelled of the outdoors, a scent more heady than any aftershave. His eyes had darkened so they resembled the kind of sinfully rich chocolate that sold for a premium price. "Why do I need to go?"

Why? Was he dense? Didn't he understand the danger he was putting them in? Didn't he foresee the monumental mess that would result if they gave in to temptation?

"I think you know very well why," she whispered.

He took another step forward, the way she wanted

to. Instead, she mustered the will to move another step backward. She was barefoot, and he was so very tall. Even his height excited her. Why had she thought he was too tall?

"Why don't you tell me why," he whispered back, "so we're clear?"

"Because," she said and lost her train of thought when she focused on his generous mouth. His lips were relaxed, soft, waiting for her to kiss them. Which she absolutely could not. She closed her eyes, thought hard and had an inspiration. "Because I have an appointment with a client."

"You do?" He scrunched up his eyebrows and checked his watch. She read the doubt on his face clearer than if he'd written the word on a chalkboard. "But it's only four o'clock. Isn't your appointment for later?"

His guess was correct, but she wasn't about to tell him that. Not when it seemed like she might make a lucky escape. "No," she said, shaking her head. "My appointment's for four-thirty."

"Four-thirty? Are you sure?"

"Perfectly sure," she said and ducked around him, almost running to the door in her desperation to get away from him. She pulled it open and let the much-needed cool air rush over her. "I'll have just enough time to change my clothes and rush over there if you leave now. My client won't be happy if I'm late."

"About this client . . ." Chase said, trailing her at a snail's pace. He obviously wasn't ready to leave.

"I hear he's an ogre. A stickler about being on time," Michelle lied. She didn't know anything at all about the client except his name was Mr. Gibson and she was supposed to meet him at six o'clock.

Chase paused at the door, and her nerve ends tingled. She needed to get him out of her townhouse. Now. Without pausing to reconsider, she did a quick maneuver to position herself behind Chase and gave him a little push toward the door.

"I can't believe he's that bad, because—"

"I'll call you later this week about when I can take Lauren to get her ears pierced," she interrupted. "Bye, Chase."

She shut the door in his surprised face and leaned against it, sucking in breath as though she'd been running too fast. Her heart, she could hear, was racing.

Sheeeesh. That had been far too close. A minute longer, and she couldn't have stopped herself from launching into his arms.

At a few minutes before six, Michelle pulled up to the curb in front of the gorgeous Cape Cod she was due to show Mr. Gibson. She'd previewed the house the week before during a realtor open house, and it was the stuff of her dreams.

Four bedrooms with walk-in closets in each one. A master bath equipped with Jacuzzi. A sunken family room with oversized fireplace. Hardwood floors. Built-in bookshelves throughout the house. All in a neighborhood so beautiful she'd be hard-pressed not to drool when she looked out the window.

Michelle told herself to stop dreaming and pushed at the door of her economical Chevy. It didn't budge. Again. Which brought home the point that she was as far away from affording a house like the Cape Cod as heaven was from earth. She only hoped Mr. Gibson turned out to have deeper pockets than she did. Much deeper pockets.

She scooted across the front seat, let herself out the passenger side and wondered about the mysterious Mr. Gibson. Since arriving in Virginia, the only way she'd picked up new clients was by sitting in the office answering the telephone. But Mr. Gibson had called while she was out and left a message that he wanted her to show him this particular house.

A stroke of luck, to be sure. The only thing she needed more than another client was a sale. Since pawning the television to help cover the last rent payment, she'd been stewing over how to make the next one. Jason had seemed to understand about the television, but would he be as sympathetic if they were evicted?

She breathed in the cool fall air and brought herself up to her full height. She wouldn't think negative thoughts, not when Mr. Gibson could turn out to be the buyer she needed.

A silver Mercedes was parked in the driveway, telling her the real-estate agent listing the house had beat her here. She was halfway up the sidewalk when from behind her came the sound of squealing tires. She turned in time to see a red Jeep bang over the curb, one of its tires skidding on grass, before coming to rest behind her Chevy.

What a madman! she thought, an instant before *her* madman stepped out of the Jeep.

Chase! What was Chase doing here?

He waved and smiled, sending another wave of longing through a body that hadn't had time to recover from their last encounter. He started toward her with that maddening amble of his, completely erasing from her mind all the high points of the house she'd wanted to hit with Mr. Gibson. This wasn't fair. She was working here.

She hurried down the sidewalk, her high heels clicking on the flagstone, and held her hand out palm up. "Stop right there, buster," she said, using her best no-nonsense voice. "You need to leave."

"But I just got here." A corner of his mouth kicked up, and she felt as though she'd been kicked in the stomach. Lord, the man could smile.

"I'm serious, Chase." She wagged a finger. "I don't know how you found out where I was, but I'm working. I know I put you off before, and I'm sorry, but you know as well as I do that we can't be alone together."

"But I'm not—"

"I mean it, Chase. You have to leave. So far we've managed not to kiss in front of the kids, but imagine how unprofessional it would be to kiss in front of a client. This Mr. Gibson could be a prude. Why, he . . ."

"I'm Mr. Gibson."

". . . could be seventy years old, for all I know about—"

"I said I'm Mr. Gibson," Chase interrupted. "I'm your six o'clock appointment."

"You're not Mr. Gibson." She put her hands on her

hips and narrowed her eyes. "Your last name's Fletcher."

"Chase Gibson Fletcher, in the flesh." He gave a little bow. "Gibson is my mother's maiden name. It's also the name I used when I called your office."

When she realized her jaw had dropped, she snapped it up again. "But I don't understand. Why didn't you tell me?"

"I tried to back at the townhouse when you were lying about the time of your appointment. But before I could get it out, you shut the door in my face."

She shook her head. "No. I meant why didn't you tell me before now? Why try to hide who you were?"

He shifted his weight from one foot to the other, looking uncomfortable. "Because I wasn't sure you'd agree to be my real-estate agent."

"Are you kidding? I'd agree to be Attila the Hun's real-estate agent as long as he promised not to pillage and plunder on my time. Why wouldn't I agree to be yours?"

"Because," he said, raising his eyebrows, "you seem to have this aversion to being alone with me inside an empty house."

One minute, her purse was hanging over her shoulder. The next, it was connecting with his chest.

"You knew," she accused.

He clutched at his chest. "How could I have known you were going to thwap me with your purse?"

"I'm not talking about that. Back at the townhouse, you knew I was afraid to be alone with you! But did you make it easier for me? Oh, no. You pretended you didn't know what I was talking about. Then I had to practically shove you out the door." Her nose twitched but it couldn't be helped. "How could you have done that?"

"Maybe," he said slowly, locking his eyes with hers, "I don't have an aversion to being alone inside a house with you."

"You do, too!" Michelle retorted and sneezed. He handed her a handkerchief and she took it absently. "You know what would happen. We wouldn't be able to keep our hands off each other. You know how disastrous that would be."

"Maybe I've had a change of heart." He shrugged. "Maybe I think we should let nature take its course."

"A change of heart?"

"That's what I said. A change of heart."

Michelle was so stunned, she couldn't speak. He didn't mean he'd had a change of heart about marrying a domestic goddess, she was sure, but that he'd changed his mind about dallying with her. He probably thought they could indulge in something quick and temporary before he got on with the rest of his life.

She gazed up at him. The sun had already faded, and his mahogany hair looked almost black in the twilight. Half of his face was in shadow, but he still looked so handsome she nearly swooned. Darn it all. Why did she always have to be so careful? Just this once, couldn't she reach for what she wanted without thinking so hard about the repercussions?

Besides, maybe there wouldn't be any repercussions. Maybe he'd be like the cotton candy she coveted whenever she went to the carnival. Her craving grew every time she walked by a booth selling the confection until she finally gave in and bought some. Every time, it was the same. One bite—one scrumptious, luscious bite—was enough.

Maybe one date—okay, two or three dates tops—with Chase would be enough, too.

"Think about it, Michelle," he continued. "It wouldn't kill us to be alone inside a couple of houses together. It might even be kind of fun."

She dabbed at her nose, only to find that it had stopped watering. He was right. They were adults who were attracted to each other. They should be able to handle a casual relationship.

"I will think about it," she said, knowing that would be practically all she thought about. "But don't get any ideas about this house. I thought I was meeting a stranger, so I asked the listing agent to be present. He's waiting for us."

Chase snapped his fingers, but his smile was good-natured. "Darn it. Why didn't I just use my real name?"

Michelle started up the flagstone sidewalk, pausing to throw a look over her shoulder. "Are you really in the market for a new house or was this a ploy to get me alone?"

"You've seen my house," Chase said, following her at a leisurely pace. "We've already outgrown it. Besides, if we get a larger place, it won't look so messy. There'd be more room to spread out the clutter."

That sounded like a valid reason to her. "Then get ready to be sold, Mr. Gibson."

*　*　*

Michelle held on tight to the arm rest inside the door of Chase's Jeep as he sent the vehicle careening around corners and barreling toward red lights. He slowed down when he should have sped up and accelerated when he should have decelerated.

The Moo Goo Gai Pan she'd eaten for dinner rolled uneasily in her stomach, and her knuckles had turned white mere seconds into the ten-minute ride. When he pulled into the residential neighborhood where they'd left her Chevy, she understood that he'd been telling the truth the first time they'd met.

He hadn't taken her parking place in the school lot by design. The miracle was that he'd been able to pull into it without hitting the adjacent cars.

"You are an unbelievably rotten driver," she said after the Jeep skidded to a sudden stop that propelled her body forward, then back.

"I am not," Chase protested.

Michelle unclenched her hands and watched as some color seeped back into her knuckles. She was about to reach inside her purse for an antacid tablet when something occurred to her. If they compromised, she wouldn't need one.

"I can go along with that," she said, "as long as you let me do the driving next time." She cut her eyes at him. "And the next time and the next."

Chase grinned and let the insult to his driving roll off. Whether she realized it or not, she'd acknowledged that she was going to stop fighting this thing between them. Otherwise, there wouldn't be so many next times.

"That's fine with me. I don't much like to drive anyway."

Her eyes narrowed. "Why are you being so agreeable?"

"I'm usually agreeable." He shrugged. "It's my nature to be agreeable."

"Does that mean you'll agree to put a bid in on the Cape Cod?" She nodded to the house, which was artfully illuminated by dramatic ground lights. "Take it from me, it won't last. If you wait too long, you'll lose it."

He laughed, remembering the gushing way she'd described each room. "It's the first house I've seen. I need to look at a few others before I decide anything. For comparison's sake, if nothing else."

"I wouldn't need to," Michelle said. "If I could afford to buy a house, this is the one I'd want."

"Spoken like a true salesman."

"In this case, it's the truth. Even before I found out you were my client, I thought Mr. Gibson had awfully good taste to pick it out."

"Lauren and I bicycle by it sometimes. I always wanted to see if it looked as good on the inside as it does on the outside."

"The outside would be even nicer with your landscaping skills." She pointed out the car window to a bare area along the front of the house. "What would you put there?"

He surveyed the area. "Probably some of the camellia bushes that are in front of your townhouse. They flower in the spring and give good color in the fall."

"See," Michelle pressed. "Imagine how much more beautiful the house will look once you plant camellia bushes and landscape the yard. It'll be stunning."

He laughed when he realized she was still playing the part of the salesman, which he had to admit she did to perfection. "Stop trying to sell me, Michelle. You're off duty, and you've just reached an important decision."

She looked surprised, adorably so. "I have?"

He nodded. "You've decided to stop fighting this thing between us."

He thought it was shock that made her blue eyes widen. "How do you know that?"

"I'm a smart guy." He managed a smile. "Besides, you just admitted it."

"So what if I did? You feel the same way," she said, sounding and looking defensive until the corners of her mouth drooped. "You do, don't you?"

"Oh, yes," he answered quickly. "Didn't you notice the death grip I had on my fork in the restaurant? I was afraid that, if I let go, we'd give the other diners a show. Not a G-rated one, either."

She didn't say anything for a moment, but her lips parted and a pulse in her neck jumped. He watched her nose for a sign he'd gone too far, but for once it didn't move. Neither did he.

"Say something, Michelle," he finally implored. "I'm dying over here."

"You're not holding a fork now," she whispered.

It was all the invitation he needed. He reached for her, wondering how he'd ever been able to resist. Since the first moment he'd seen her, wet and bedraggled in Principal Goodman's office, he'd had to exercise superhuman control to stop himself from reaching for her.

At the first touch of her lips on his, he spiraled out of control. She kissed him softly, sweetly, nipping at his lower lip and giving him silent permission to deepen the kiss by opening her mouth. He took it gladly, his tongue swirling with hers in perfect, passionate harmony. In the recesses of his mind it occurred to him that they'd both known all along that this is how it would be between them.

Something hard and unyielding jammed his ribs, and he yelped. The steering wheel. "Owww," he said, his mouth still on hers. "Whoever got rid of bench seats should be shot."

She laughed against his mouth, sending little vibrations across his lips.

"There's more room over here in my seat than yours," she said, wondering where she'd gotten the nerve to issue the invitation. The thought left her mind an instant later as he bumped elbow, knee and his rib again in his eagerness to comply. She was laughing by the time he ended up in her seat, somehow, with her on his lap.

"So you think I'm funny, do you?" he asked, smiling at her while placing his hands on her waist.

She smiled back, cupping his face in her hands. "I think," she said, "you're wonderful."

Then she kissed him, giving herself over to him, giving herself over to passion. He kissed the way he moved, slowly, leisurely, as though they had all the time in the world. Only his heartbeat was fast. She strained to get closer to him, wondering why she'd tried so hard to stay away.

It had never been this way for her. Not even in college when she'd been dazzled by Jason's father. Jason. On the edges of her mind, she realized there was something she needed to remember about Jason. She drew back slightly from his lips.

"Chase?" she said, but he only drew her forward again, kissing her so thoroughly her head spun. She was dimly aware of the windows fogging, of the fact that they were necking in the residential neighborhood where she was trying to sell a house.

"Chase, we've got to stop," she said again when his lips moved to her neck. Pinpricks of desire coursed through her.

"Why?" he asked as his mouth moved to her ear. She shivered.

"Because, if we don't, your soon-to-be neighbors might call the cops on us."

"Bad reason," he whispered in her ear. She shivered again.

"And I'm already late in picking up Jason."

He leaned back against the head rest, and his arms loosened. She could hear him trying to get his breathing back under control. "If you don't get out of this car in the next second, I can't be held responsible for my actions."

She giggled and reached for the door handle, scrambling off his lap. Chase was such a gentleman she wasn't afraid he'd make good on his threat. She was afraid she'd change her mind and jump back onto his lap. She leaned over and gave him a quick kiss on the lips.

"Witch," he teased when she drew back, but it was an insult she savored.

She replayed their interlude in her mind during the entire drive to Dani White's house, like a young girl after her first date. She laughed aloud. She felt like a teenager. Tingly and excited and happy.

When she pulled up in front of Dani White's house, the truth hit her so hard that, for a moment, she couldn't breathe. This euphoria racing through her could only mean one thing.

She leaned her forehead on the steering wheel as the folly of what she'd done raced through her limp body.

Despite her best efforts, she'd gone and fallen in love with Chase Fletcher.

Chapter Nine

Chase put his hands behind his neck and settled deeper into the comfortable sofa as he watched Sports Center on the new thirty-two-inch television set in Michelle's townhouse.

It was nearly ten o'clock, and Jason was asleep in his bedroom. Michelle had called Chase on his cell phone hours ago when he and Jason were at a baseball-card show, spewing apologies because she'd been called into work by clients who wanted to bid on a house.

Chase had told her he'd watch Jason for as long as her business took and gone on to enjoy an evening filled with takeout pizza, pro wrestling and good company. Jason and Lauren had fought over the pieces of pizza with the most pepperoni and rooted for different wrestlers, but Chase was encouraged that neither of them had been inspired to body slam the other.

One hour had stretched into two, then three, until Chase had finally left Lauren with his father and driven an exhausted Jason home.

He stretched, hit the mute button on the television remote and got up to put a CD on Michelle's stereo. Soft music drifted through the room as peace filled his soul. He hadn't been exaggerating when he told Michelle he was content to wait as long as her business took. Because she was coming home. To him.

He smiled to himself. He and Michelle had managed to see each other four of the last five days, although they'd had precious little time alone. A pair of eleven-year-olds, he'd discovered, made better chaperons than a circa-1800s maiden aunt.

But even that was okay. Chase had never been one to rush things, preferring instead to wait for what he wanted. Somewhere between being blasted with insults at the principal's office and now, he'd figured out he wanted more than a couple of kisses from Michelle.

Oh, he wanted those kisses. Wanted them and much, much more quite desperately. But he could as easily envision Michelle in his future as in his arms. When he'd met Michelle, he'd pegged her as a driven career woman along the mold of his ex-wife. The type of woman who burned him once and would never get a chance to again. But now he was reconsidering his first impression.

Michelle twanged with tension every time she mentioned real estate, not the best indicator of a love affair with her job. Nobody chose that kind of high-stress life by choice.

Now that he'd seen how wonderful she was with

her son and his daughter, he figured she'd happily ditch the job in favor of family when he asked her to marry him.

To marry him?

For a moment, Chase couldn't move. He couldn't even breathe. The idea that he wanted to marry Michelle must have been rolling around in his brain for the past week or even longer, but he hadn't consciously thought it until now.

He drew a breath, flooding his lungs with air, flooding himself with the certainty that marrying Michelle was exactly what he wanted to do. Sure, she could anger him as easily as arouse him. And sure, she was having a hard time relying on anyone but herself. But they could work on those things.

Especially because he loved her.

Before he could get used to that truth, keys jangled in the lock on the front door, signaling Michelle's return.

His breathing back under control, Chase rose from the sofa. Now was the time to think about her needs, not his. After working so late, Michelle was sure to be mentally and physically exhausted. She'd need somebody to help her wind down from the pressures of her too-demanding profession, and he was the man for the job.

He put on a sympathetic expression as the door opened, but was unprepared for the sight of Michelle bursting through it. She always looked lovely, but a special radiance about her tonight made his breath hitch. An aura of energy surrounded her like a bright light. Her white teeth flashed, her skin glowed and her eyes shone.

She bumped the door closed with her hip, dropped her briefcase, raised her arms overhead and did a graceful pirouette. Her blond hair and the short, flared skirt of her suit twirled with her. Then she laughed her sexy, throaty laugh.

"Congratulations are in order," she said and whirled again.

"Congratulations for what?" Chase asked, smiling.

She rushed to his side and tilted her head back to look at him, her blue eyes as bright as a shimmering sea. She laid a long-fingered hand, its nails painted deep pink, on his arm.

"Oh, Chase, I had the best day," she said. "Do you realize I only met that couple I told you about on the phone yesterday at an open house? When I showed them that Colonial this afternoon, I just knew they were going to offer for it. And they did!"

She let out a giddy little sound, somewhere between a giggle and a cry of triumph. "Here's the cool part. The owners didn't accept their first offer, but I convinced the buyers to take out the clause demanding the washer and dryer stay and to counter with a bid a thousand dollars higher. And guess what?"

"They went for it," Chase finished.

"They went for it. And, voila, we had a sale." She clapped, twirled again and collapsed onto the sofa. "Isn't that wonderful?"

"Well, yes," he said, but he couldn't stop from frowning. This wasn't at all what he'd expected while he sat waiting for her. He thought she'd come in the door popping antacid tablets and suffering from one of her headaches. Instead, she was exhilarated, the way his attorney ex-wife had been when she won a case.

"You're right. It is wonderful," she said, leaning back against the sofa and smiling. Her blond hair spread out behind her like a crown of light. She didn't look like a woman who'd give up her job tomorrow for a chance at domestic bliss. She threw her head back and laughed. "I absolutely adore this job."

Chase's throat closed, and his heartbeat slowed to a painful thump. He stuffed his hands in the pockets of his trousers, hoping he hadn't heard her correctly but knowing he had.

"You were telling the truth at the science museum when you said you liked your job, weren't you?"

She gazed up from the sofa with a bemused smile, as though he'd asked if she'd lied about loving her son. Or being female.

"Of course I was telling the truth," she said. "I don't just like my job. I love it. It has its share of pressure, sure, but there's nothing like making a sale. It's an incredible high."

Nothing beats winning a case. It's an unbelievable rush.

His ex-wife's voice came back to him, making what Michelle had said sound distressingly familiar. His shoulders slumped. Michelle's real-estate career obviously meant as much to her as the law profession did to Andrea.

"Chase, is something wrong?" Michelle sat up, suddenly alert. Her features pinched with concern. "It's not Jason, is it? Is there something you're not telling me?"

"Jason's fine," he said, then lied. "And nothing's wrong."

"Thank God." She expelled a breath. "I shouldn't have left him with you for so long. I didn't mean to. It took longer than I thought, but he would have been fine if he'd come with me."

"Stop it, Michelle. You don't hear me complaining, do you?"

"Of course you wouldn't, but I still shouldn't have—"

"I said stop it," Chase repeated, trying to process what he'd learned. Michelle loved her job. Just like Andrea had loved hers. But maybe he could work with that. Andrea had never needed him, but Michelle and Jason did. He forced himself to keep his tone of voice normal. "Jason's a great kid, and we had a good time. We watched pro wrestling with Lauren and my dad, and we ate pizza."

Michelle picked her purse off the coffee table where she'd dropped it and rooted through it for her wallet. "Let me give you some money to cover Jason's share." She pulled out a bill. "Will this do it?"

Chase's muscles tensed, and the hairs on the back of his neck stood up. He felt like the world he'd been living in during the past week, the one where he and Michelle had forged a partnership, was crumbling around him. But maybe that world had existed only in his mind.

"I thought we got this straight at the baseball field," Chase said through clenched teeth. "You're not paying me for spending time with Jason."

"But you keep buying him tokens at the batting cage, and pizza costs—"

"Would you stop it?" He took the bill from her and shoved it back in her purse. "I'm not taking your money."

"Okay," Michelle said and sat back on the sofa, surprising him. He felt a flare of hope that she'd finally relaxed her guard long enough to let him help her. Then her eyes flicked to the glowing picture on the television set, and he knew the next few minutes would define their relationship.

"What's that?" Accusation tinged her voice.

"It's your television."

"Oh, no." Michelle gave a vehement shake of her head. "I don't have a television anymore. And the one I did have certainly wasn't that big."

"That's because I bought this one for you today."

Michelle stood up. They were separated by just inches. Color suffused her face, but she kept her voice level. "Jason told you I was having trouble making the rent, didn't he?"

"So what if he did? It's something you should have told me yourself."

"Oh. And why's that?"

"So I could help you. And don't tell me you don't need any help, because I've already helped." He lifted his chin, knowing how much was riding on the next statement. "I didn't want you to have to pawn anything else, so I paid next month's rent for you."

"You what?"

"I said I paid next month's rent."

The words dangled between them. Like bait, Chase

thought. Would she take it for what it was: a sincere effort to make her life easier by the man who'd fallen for her? Or would she spit it back at him?

"Let me get this straight. You won't take money from me for the pizza Jason ate, but I'm supposed to take a television set and money for rent from you?" She tapped a finger against her cheek in a gesture that made it appear as though she was deep in thought. Her nose quivered, and Chase knew better. She'd already decided exactly what she thought.

"That's not a fair comparison," he said. "I'm not the one having financial problems."

"That's just it." She sneezed. "It's my problem, not yours."

He stung as much as if she was throwing darts at him instead of words. Had he really thought she'd give up even a fraction of her precious independence and learn to rely on him? Had he really believed they could make not only a relationship, but a marriage, work? Fool that he was beginning to think he was, he still held out hope that he could make her see how good it could be between them.

"I thought," he said tightly, "we'd progressed to the point where it was *our* problem."

"Why would you think that?"

"Because, damn it, I care about you, Michelle." He grabbed her by the shoulders. His muscles strained with the effort not to pull her soft body flush against his. His breath burned like fire in his lungs. He'd almost said he loved her, but he was afraid to push any more than he already was. "I thought you cared about me, too."

Cared about him? Michelle almost laughed at the understatement. She loved him. The truth must have flickered in her eyes, because his hands left her shoulders and he cupped her face, tilting it toward his.

"This could work, Michelle. I make enough to support all of us. You, me, Lauren, Jason, even my dad. You wouldn't have to work if you didn't want to."

Not have to work? The bottom dropped out of Michelle's stomach. He didn't understand her at all. Not only did she love her job, but it was essential to the fabric of her life. If she didn't work, she wouldn't have a means of supporting Jason and herself. And, if she didn't have a means of support, she wouldn't have anything to fall back on if Chase suddenly decided he'd had enough of them.

Men left. Sooner or later, Chase would too.

"Say something, Michelle," he implored.

"I'm taking the TV back and I'm getting your check back from my landlord. You haven't been listening to me, Chase. I just made a sale. I can do this by myself. I don't need your money."

"This isn't about money. This is about you and me. About us."

"There is no us," she said while her heart screamed that wasn't true. "I don't need you, and neither does my son."

She took a step backward, and his hands dropped from her face. He looked like somebody had punched him in the gut. She wanted to take him in her arms and soothe the hurt by telling him she hadn't meant what she said, but she couldn't take the risk any more than she could let herself need him.

"Do you really believe that?" he asked after a moment. His voice sounded thick. "Or are you afraid to admit to yourself that Jason needs a father and you need somebody to help you out?"

"Is that why you hired me to find a house for you, Chase? Because you wanted to help me out?"

"That's not what—"

"Is that what you'd do if we were together? Help me out by having me quit my job so I could become that domestic goddess you want?"

"What I want has—"

"Because you can forget it. I'm never quitting my job and putting myself in a position where I have to rely on somebody else. I can't be the woman you want."

They stared at each other for long, silent moments. Despite what she'd said, it took all Michelle's willpower not to walk into his arms and rejoice that he cared enough to want to help her. But she didn't. Finally, he shook his head in what looked like disgust and threw up his hands.

"I don't know why I thought we could make this thing between us work," he bit out. "Go ahead and work sixty hours a week if it makes you happy."

He turned and headed for the door, and she had to bite down on her bottom lip to keep from calling him back. When he was gone, her rubbery legs could no longer support her and she collapsed onto the sofa. Tears fell like rain down her cheeks.

What had begun as a night of promise had dimmed to despair. The commission she'd make on the house she sold tonight would help her get out of her financial rut, which should have been cause for celebration.

But Michelle didn't feel like celebrating. All she felt was a yawning emptiness.

Chapter Ten

Orange and black crepe paper streamed from the rafters of the Starlight Pond gymnasium. Between the strands, snowy-white ghosts and inky-black bats floated above the crowd. Below, witches mingled with angels and devils consorted with princesses.

Chase, dressed all in black, adjusted his long, dark cape around himself and dropped his fangs into his pocket. He'd been such a bust at the last event he'd chaperoned he figured he might as well take full advantage of the fact that this was a Halloween dance.

He'd already put the fangs to good use once when he scolded Dinosaur Boy for trying to swallow classmates with his fake Tyrannosaurus Rex head.

Telling misbehaving children he was going to drain them of blood if they didn't shape up worked surprisingly well.

He wondered if that tactic would have worked on

Michelle two weeks ago when she'd told him she wanted him out of her life.

Let me in, he could have said, *or I'll suck your blood*.

He sighed and leaned against the wall adjacent to the punch bowl, which was filled with a syrupy orange liquid. For two weeks, he'd tried not to think about Michelle. For two weeks, he'd failed. She crept into his thoughts in the day, when he was supposed to be drawing up site plans for a new county park, and stayed in them at night so he had a hard time sleeping.

He'd picked up the phone to call her a dozen times, only to hang it up again when he realized they didn't have anything to talk about. She wouldn't let herself care about him, and he couldn't keep pursuing a woman as wrapped up in her career as his ex-wife was in hers.

Something tickled his nose, and he flinched, only to feel foolish when he realized it was a plastic spider suspended from the ceiling by a thread.

"Let me take care of that little nuisance for you," said a voice in a very bad British accent. A gloved hand carrying a white handkerchief appeared before his eyes and whisked the spider away.

He looked down into the laughing, rosy-cheeked face of Dani White. She wore a black felt hat atop hair pulled back into a no-nonsense bun. Her fitted coat was black and covered a long skirt and white blouse. A jaunty orange scarf was tied at her neck.

"Mary Poppins, I presume," Chase said, smiling.

She tapped the tip of her black umbrella on the gymnasium floor. "A very astute observation," she said with her atrocious British accent, then laughed. "I thought I should come as an authority figure since there are forty sixth-graders and only four of us."

"Four chaperons?" Chase screwed up his forehead. "I only see three."

"No, there's four. I should know. I made the arrangements." Dani pointed to Principal Goodman, who was wearing running shoes and jogging in place to the dark, creepy music that was being broadcast through a loud speaker. He had on a tank top and silky, high-cut shorts that called attention to his skinny legs. "Besides you and me, there's Thurman, who's a marathoner. And Michelle." Dani squinted in the direction of the dance floor. "Except I can't tell what she is."

Chase straightened all the way from the wall and immediately spotted Michelle. She must have just arrived, because he wouldn't have missed her had she been there earlier. She'd sprinkled gold dust through hair that fell in rivulets around her heart-shaped face, and she was wearing a pale yellow chiffon ball gown with a tight-fitting bodice that made his blood quicken. Despite the heat flowing through his veins, he had to smile. Nobody could accuse Michelle of not having a sense of humor.

"She's the belle of the ball," Chase said. *La Belle Michelle.*

Dani put her hands on her hips. There was such a twinkle in her eyes that, for a moment, she really did resemble the fictional character she was portraying. "Now how would you know that?"

"I'm Count Dracula," he said. "I know all."

"All Count Dracula knows how to do is draw

blood," Dani countered, then gave a loud sigh. Her son, Benny Joe, dressed as a pirate, was clanking plastic swords with Zorro. "Save me a dance for later, if you're free. I've got to break this up."

She walked away on black-booted feet, clapping her white-gloved hands. "Spit spot, children. Holster your swords. Remember the innocent bystanders."

Chase hardly noticed her retreat, because his attention was riveted by Michelle. She laughed at something a girl dressed as Dorothy from the Wizard of Oz said, cocking her head so he could see the creamy smoothness of her skin. He wanted to put his mouth on her neck so badly his lips ached along with the rest of him.

She turned then, and their eyes locked. Everything else, even the flashing orange florescent lights, faded to black. For an instant, it seemed as though they were the only two people in the room. Attraction zinged through him, as though he'd been zapped with a live wire. His heart throbbed heavily in his chest.

He couldn't remember why he shouldn't cross the room and take her into his arms until somebody tapped her on the arm and she broke eye contact. Then he remembered. Even if she hadn't dumped him, it wouldn't have worked out between them. Her job had seen to that.

"Are you okay, Chase?" a young voice asked. "You look a little funny."

"That's because I'm Count Dracula. I'm supposed to look funny," Chase said, dramatically swinging his robe around him as he turned. Jason looked up at him, grinning.

"Speaking of looking funny," Chase said. "Look at you."

Jason had on a red batting helmet, high-top red shoes and a white baseball uniform sporting the number twenty-five. But that wasn't what made him look funny. The material he'd stuffed under his baseball shirt did that. Chase poked at Jason's shirt, and it sprang back like it was alive.

"Let me guess," Chase said, chuckling. "You're Mark McGwire, and those rubber balloons are your muscles."

"Bingo." Jason flexed his balloons. "You need gigantic muscles to be a home-run king."

A wave of affection washed over Chase as Jason went through more muscle-man poses. Although Michelle had been emphatic when she insisted Jason didn't need him, she hadn't put a stop to their weekly trips to the batting cage. Still, he wasn't spending nearly as much time with Jason as he would have liked.

"Everybody loves a slugger," Chase said. "I bet no girl in the place would say no if you asked her to dance."

Chase expected Jason to reject the suggestion, but instead he scuffed his high-top shoe on the gym floor. "Yeah. Too bad I can't dance."

The boy's expression was so downcast that Chase had to do something to lift it. "Tell you what. I'm not an expert, but I could show you a couple steps if you want. We could go out in the hall where no one would see."

"Really?" Jason's expression lightened. "Would you really do that for me?"

Chase slung an arm around the boy's shoulder. "I'd do just about anything for you, sport," he said, knowing that he could have made the same statement to Jason's mother.

Too bad, he thought sadly, she wasn't going to give him the chance.

Michelle needed air.

She tried to convince herself it was because the bodice of her dress was drawn too tightly around her ribs, but she suspected the real reason was Count Dracula.

Since spotting Chase in his vampire costume, she'd barely been able to function. Who'd have thought the Count could be such a hunk? Or that she'd be so mixed up over having told the hunk to take a hike?

She'd lost sight of him after Lucifer asked her to pin on his devil's tail. Since she wanted to avoid him, she should have been grateful. Instead, she'd craned her neck this way and that trying to spot him.

It was pathetic, is what it was. Had she known he'd be here, she would have refused Dani White's request that she be a chaperon. But now that he was here, she was almost sick with anxiety. Who knew what crazy thing she might do if she ran into him?

Her skirts rustling behind her, Michelle headed for the gymnasium exit closest to her. It led to an interior hallway instead of the outdoors, which wasn't ideal but would have to do. She pushed the door open and froze.

Halfway down the hall, a tall man in a vampire suit

and a boy in a baseball uniform were so deep in concentration that neither noticed her. Chase and Jason. Chase rested his large hand on the back of Jason's baseball shirt, and Michelle's throat closed.

"Okay, take a big step, then a little step," Chase said. "One, two. One, two. That's it. You're getting it."

Michelle's lips parted in awe. Chase was teaching Jason how to slow dance. It was the kind of thing a father would do, and she couldn't imagine a better father than Chase. Considering how much Jason talked about Chase, she knew her son shared that opinion.

In that instant, she also knew she'd been deluding herself when she claimed Jason didn't need Chase. Chase was exactly what Jason needed.

Slowly, before either male saw her, Michelle backed away. She slipped into the gym, dazed by what she'd seen and what she'd realized, and ran smack into Lauren.

"Oh, Michelle. I'm so glad I found you," the girl said. She was dressed in a beautiful white gown with blue beading. Tiny fake diamond earrings adorned her newly pierced ears. She waved something, and Michelle saw it was a tiara. "This dang thing won't stay on. I tried to get Dad to put my hair up, but he did such a lousy job it fell out as soon as we got here."

Michelle took the tiara and laid a hand on Lauren's shoulder. Oh, to be so young that your biggest concern was a tiara that wouldn't stick instead of a man you couldn't love.

"I'll fix you right up, Cinderella," Michelle said. "Do you have anything I can tie your hair up with?"

The girl handed her some elastics and bobby pins. Michelle made some deft moves, gave a couple of twists and had Lauren's hair in a topknot within a few moments. The tiara stuck like glue. "There. Now you can go to the ball and find Prince Charming."

"You mean you're done? Already?" Lauren's grin spread. "How does it look?"

"As beautiful as you do. The boys will be begging you for a dance," Michelle teased. Instead of denying she wanted to dance with a boy, as Michelle had expected, Lauren looked hopeful.

"Do you really think so, Michelle? Oh, I hope he asks me."

Before Michelle could ask what particular boy she had in mind, Chase and Jason came back into the gym. Michelle took a step backward into the shadows and watched as Dani White whisked across the dance floor holding out a white-gloved hand to Chase. He took it as the music changed from a fast-moving rock song to a slow ballad.

Dani's clothes were so much like the ones Julie Andrews had worn in the Mary Poppins movie that Michelle suspected she'd sewn the costume herself. She watched as Dani linked her hands around Chase's neck and thought she was going to be sick.

In one of her hands, Dani held a measuring tape. Michelle had watched the movie enough times that she remembered the scene in which Mary Poppins had taken her own measurement and read the tape aloud to her charges: *Practically perfect in every way.*

That saying applied to Dani White, the epitome of a domestic goddess, as much as it did to Mary Poppins. Except Dani was practically perfect in every way for Chase, the man Michelle loved.

Horror washed over her as she realized she had driven Chase into Dani's arms. He'd been ready to propose just two weeks ago, but she'd stubbornly refused to let him past the wall she'd erected to protect herself and Jason from getting hurt. She'd refused to consider she needed him every bit as much as her son did. Maybe even more.

She needed to hear his slow, even breathing while he slept next to her. Needed to have his support when life wasn't going her way. Needed him to rejoice with her over her successes. Needed to share his daughter and his life.

Denying those needs had only made her miserable. That's why her spirits had been so low when they should have been sky-high over her recent real-estate triumphs and improving relationship with Jason.

Life was empty when you couldn't share it with someone you loved.

She wanted to shout her newfound knowledge to the Starlight Pond crowd, to rush across the dance floor and fling herself into Chase's arms.

Except she couldn't, because she'd already lost him.

"Michelle?" Lauren was gazing at her with concern. "Are you okay?"

"No. I mean yes." Michelle touched Lauren's cheek. She didn't want to worry the girl, especially because Lauren already had claimed a place in Michelle's heart. Right next to the one Chase occupied. "I'm just going to go outside a few minutes for some air."

"Do you want me to come with you?"

"No, honey." She forced herself to smile. The dance was full of possibilities for Lauren, and the girl needed her encouragement to snatch one of them. "If that boy doesn't ask you to dance, ask him. If you're too afraid to grab what you want today, by tomorrow it might be gone."

"Huh?" Lauren asked, but Michelle had already swept by her, intent on the cover of night. She didn't spare another glance at Chase, who was watching her intently over the top of Dani White's head. Where, he wondered, was Michelle going? And why did she look so upset?

"Then I found a pattern at the fabric store I knew would be perfect for Benny Joe's pirate costume." Dani chattered on, oblivious to the fact that he was only half listening. Could Michelle have been upset because he was dancing with Dani? "But I had a devil of a time finding the right material for his pants until it occurred to me that the curtains in the living room were perfect. They're made of broadcloth."

He gave her an absent smile, still only half paying attention. But it didn't make sense that Michelle would be jealous of Dani, who he'd never thought of as anything other than a friend.

"So I went hunting for new curtains and made Benny Joe's pirate breeches out of the old ones." Dani laughed, although Chase hadn't heard her say anything funny. "Then it dawned on me that's what I sometimes do with my recipes. If I don't have the right ingredients in the house, I use what's on hand. I'm so domestic sometimes it scares even me."

Domestic? Chase considered the woman in his arms

with new eyes. Dani *was* domestic. In fact, she was the most domestic woman he knew. Some people might even refer to her as a domestic goddess, which is exactly the kind of woman he'd told Michelle he was looking for.

Except he didn't want to marry Dani. He liked her. He admired the way she'd run her family after her husband died. He enjoyed her cooking and liked visiting her spanking clean house. But he didn't love her.

He loved Michelle.

Michelle, who'd always seemed a little miffed when he talked to Dani. Michelle, who'd probably realized the other woman was a domestic goddess long before he had. Michelle, who he hoped like hell had rushed out of the dance because she was jealous.

"Would you excuse me for a minute, Dani?" he asked while he wondered which exit Michelle had taken.

"She went that way," Dani said, pointing to the exit that led to the parking lot.

"Excuse me?" Chase said.

"Michelle went that way." Dani stepped back from his arms and put her hands on her hips. "I know you two have a thing for each other. Why else did you think I talked both of you into being chaperons? Let me tell you. Thurman was not happy about it. He calls you the Dreadful Duo. He even threatened to break our date for tomorrow night over it."

Chase gaped at her, not sure whether he was more surprised at her first revelation or her second. "You're dating Principal Goodman?"

"For the past three months. And don't worry. I can

handle him." He continued to stare at her, wondering at his woeful powers of observation, until she clapped her gloved hands. "What are you waiting for, Chase? Spit spot. Go after her."

She didn't need to tell him twice. With his black cloak floating behind him, Chase hurried for the exit Dani had indicated. The night air hit his face like a cool slap, alerting him to the possibility that he could be wrong about Michelle. Seeing Dani White in his arms might not have meant a thing to her, but he had to find out.

He searched the small parking lot for Michelle's Chevy, afraid she'd already driven off, then relaxed marginally when he spotted it under the glow of a streetlight. Where could she have gone? It was a clear night, with a full moon lighting the night and stars more plentiful than they had been the night he and Michelle had sat in the planetarium under the artificial sky. He scanned the highway adjacent to the school, but didn't see anything except cars whizzing by. So he turned in the opposite direction and walked around the school building.

Fallen leaves and small twigs crunched under his shoes as he walked and scanned the area for a golden-gowned beauty. He was beginning to think he'd guessed wrong about which direction she'd taken when he spotted her sitting on a bench beside the monkey bars.

"Michelle?"

Her name rang out in the cool air. For a moment, because it sounded as though Chase had spoken it, Michelle thought she was imagining things. Then she looked up and saw him coming toward her: tall, handsome and so impossibly dear.

She wondered if Dani was inside waiting for him and glanced quickly away before he saw the need she felt sure was in her eyes. Maybe if she ignored him, he'd go away. She heard the soft footfall of his steps, and that hope vanished.

"What's the belle of the ball doing outside all by herself?"

So he'd recognized her costume. Everybody else had thought she was Cinderella or Snow White, but Chase had known differently. She wondered if she'd subconsciously dressed this way hoping she'd run into him so they could share their private joke.

"I could ask you the same thing," she said, mostly because she didn't want to answer his question. Her voice quivered. "You're supposed to be chaperoning the dance."

"You are, too," he pointed out. Without asking, he took off his cloak and draped it over her shoulders. It was a chilly night, and he probably thought she was cold. Thank goodness he didn't know her voice shook because she was upset.

"Yeah, well, I don't seem to make the greatest chaperon," she said as he sat down on the bench next to her. It was a long bench, but he chose a spot no more than six inches from her. She would have scooted over, but she was already sitting near the edge. She forced herself to forget about how near he was and to focus on reality. Dani White was reality. "You'd think Dani would have figured that out by now."

"Dani is a wonderful woman."

His words cut into Michelle. So she'd been right about Chase and Ms. Practically-Perfect-in-Every-Way. It didn't matter at the moment that Dani was her friend and she should be pleased that she was moving on after her husband's death. Michelle couldn't remember when being right had hurt more.

"If Dani is so wonderful, why aren't you inside the dance with her instead of being out here with me?" Traitorous moisture sprang to her eyes, and she wiped it away. When she looked up at him, he was smiling.

"You're jealous," he accused.

The green monster had her so firmly in its grip that she felt paralyzed, but she denied it anyway. She still had her pride. "I am not jealous. I'm angry because you think I'm jealous."

"Then why aren't you sneezing? If you were angry, you'd be sneezing. And, if you're not jealous, why did you rush out of the gym when you saw me dancing with Dani?"

"Listen, Buster," she said as she waited in vain for her nose to twitch. Why couldn't he leave her alone with her misery? "Just because I rushed out of the gym doesn't mean it had anything to do with you."

"What if I wanted it to?" he asked softly.

"It's just like you, as egotistical as you are, to assume that I was running because of you. Maybe I needed a little exercise."

To her horror, the moisture that had gathered in her eyes seeped onto her cheeks. She wanted to pretend it was because she'd come up with such an unbelievable excuse, but she knew that wasn't the reason. She couldn't even muster the will to protest when he took out a handkerchief and gently dabbed at her face. Only then did his last words register. "What did you just say?"

"I said what if I wanted the fact that you rushed out of the gym to have something to do with me?"

She stared at him for a pregnant minute, then shrugged her shoulders in defeat. She'd realized tonight she both loved and needed him, but that didn't change the fundamental fact that she wasn't the woman he was looking for. She couldn't change herself into a domestic goddess any more than he could bite her neck and transform her into a creature of the night.

"It wouldn't matter," she said sadly, and stared down at the ground.

He shoved the handkerchief back in his pocket and inched over on the bench. Cupping one side of her face, he turned her head so she had to look at him. The full moon shone down on his face, and his brown eyes burned with emotion. She wasn't sure which emotion until he spoke.

"Would it matter if I told you I love you?"

He loved her. Michelle let the sweet knowledge flow through her for a moment before she ruthlessly dismissed it.

"What about Dani?"

"My being in love with you has nothing to do with Dani, who, by the way, is dating Principal Goodman." He was looking at her so intently with eyes so tender that she could no longer doubt him. She blinked rapidly so no more tears would fall.

"You didn't answer me," he prodded gently. "Does it change things to know I love you?"

Michelle's lips trembled. "No," she said, shaking her head. "It doesn't change anything."

He let out a short, harsh sound. "Are you saying you don't love me back?"

"Of course I love you back," she snapped, appalled at the question. "I didn't want to fall in love with you, but I did. I do."

His hand fell from her face, and his jaw hardened. His mouth, she saw, was trembling. "Oh, I get it. We're back to the same old thing again, aren't we? You love me, but you don't need me."

"You *don't* get it," she said. Her nose was still. She wasn't angry, just sad. She finally understood she and Chase could be stronger together than they were apart, but that didn't change the fact that she couldn't have him. "I do need you. Oh, not to pay my bills or anything like that. I need you to love me and make my life complete."

The hope that leapt into his eyes would have been heartening if their situation wasn't so hopeless.

"Then what's the problem?" he asked.

She wrapped his cloak tighter around herself. It smelled of him, and she wished he was inside it with her. But she couldn't let that happen, not when her next words would forever shatter whatever illusions he might have about her. She took a deep breath for courage.

"You want a wife who'll stay home, and I don't blame you. Being a homemaker is an admirable calling, but that's not me. I love my son, Chase. And I love your daughter. But I love my job, too. I'm not going to quit it." Her voice lowered a notch, and her chin dipped. "Not even for you."

She waited for his response, not even sure he'd make one. She wouldn't have been surprised had he taken his cloak and disappeared into the darkness, like the creature of the night he was pretending to be. Instead, he said, "I don't want you to quit your job."

"What?" Her head snapped up. To her surprise, he was smiling.

"I realized when I was dancing with Dani that she was everything I thought I wanted. Except I didn't love her. I love you." He drew her into his arms and regarded her with eyes that sparkled. "I love how you've managed to make it on your own. I love what a good mother you are to Jason. I love how you always put your son before your job. I even love how good you are at selling real estate."

"Really?" Michelle could hardly speak through the happiness welling in her throat, but she needed to understand. "I thought you hated my job."

"When I saw first hand what a good saleswoman you are, I was proud of you. My ex-wife put work first. You don't. You put family first." Tears seeped from her eyes and he kissed her cheeks, soaking up the moisture. "It isn't your job I want you to give up, Michelle. It's your independence. I want to be dependent on you, and I want you to be dependent on me. I want us to be partners."

"That's what I want, too," Michelle whispered as she threaded her fingers through his thick, dark hair.

"I was so afraid you were like my ex-husband that I wouldn't let myself see you as you really are."

"Oh?" His eyebrows raised. "And how am I?"

"Dependable and trustworthy," she answered. "I know you won't leave us."

"Leave you? I'm never letting you go," he said as his arms tightened around her. "But now that I have you where I want you, I should confess I'd rather you didn't work sixty hours a week."

"Then I should confess that I'd be happy working forty hours a week. Or even thirty, if it meant I could spend more time with you and the kids."

"Oh, no. I don't want you to cut back on your hours just yet," he said, and her eyes widened in surprise. "Not until you sell me that Cape Cod you like so much."

"You're going to buy it? Really?"

"On one condition." He smoothed a wayward piece of hair back from her face and grew solemn. "You and Jason need to live there with me and Lauren. Marry me, Michelle. Marry me and make me whole."

The tears that had gathered in the back of her eyes fell in earnest now, but Michelle ignored them, pulling his head down to hers.

"Just you try to stop me," she said a moment before their lips met.

Much later, they walked hand in hand to the gymnasium, grinning and giggling. "Do you think Jason and Lauren will freak out when we tell them the good news?" Michelle asked.

He bent down and kissed the tip of her nose. "Anything's possible, but they've been getting along okay lately. They might surprise us."

Minutes later, they stood at the edge of the Halloween crowd, searching for their children. Michelle saw them first and might have fallen over if Chase's arm hadn't been around her.

"Am I seeing things," she asked, "or are Jason and Lauren really slow dancing?"

"Talk about surprises," Chase muttered.

Michelle's hand flew to her mouth. "Oh, my heavens. Jason must be the boy Lauren wanted to ask her to dance."

"That means Lauren is the reason Jason wanted to learn," Chase said.

As their parents watched, the young couple danced directly under the glow of an orange florescent light. Lauren gave Jason a flirtatious grin, and then, incredibly, Jason's head moved fractionally forward.

"Oh, my gosh. They're going to kiss," Michelle said in horror. "Please tell me I'm imagining this."

She held her breath, waiting for the moment the children's mouths would make impact, readying herself to run across the dance floor and pull them apart. Jason's lips moved, not toward Lauren's, but in speech. They were too far away to hear what he said, but whatever it was obviously didn't agree with Lauren.

She reared back, made a fist and slugged Jason in the shoulder. Then she stalked away. Jason rubbed his shoulder as he watched her go, his expression mutinous.

"That proves one thing, Belle," Chase said, leaning

over to whisper in her ear. His breath tickled her neck. "Our life together definitely isn't going to be boring."

She turned her head, met his lips and told him without words exactly how much she agreed.